Outlaw
Chick

Al-Saadiq Banks

i

True 2 Life Publications Presents:
Outlaw Chick

Author: Al- Saadiq Banks
Editing/Typesetting: www.21StreetUrbanEditing.com

<u>Contact Information</u>
Mail: True 2 Life Publications
PO Box 8722
Newark NJ 07108

Email: alsaadiqbanks@aol.com

Twitter: @alsaadiq

IG: @alsaadiqbanks

www.True2LifeProductions.com

ONE

Not even a hundred feet away from the highway ramp there's a Dodge mini-van which sits almost unnoticed. The many people passing by have not a clue of the magnitude of the business deal which is transacting right under their noses. Inside the van sits a Dominican in the passenger's seat as well as a Dominican in the driver's seat. In the backseat sits one of the slimiest dudes to ever step foot in the city of Newark.

This 25 year old man goes by the name of Bugsy 2 Gunz. Those that have known him since he was a child call him Bugsy. Others call him 2 Gunz, a named he earned as an adult. Whether truly knowing him or barely knowing him, when the name Bugsy 2 Gunz is mentioned, most know it normally meant chaos in the making.

Bugsy is what some may call a master of deception. Judging by face value, one may view him as a pretty boy, ladies' man. His smooth brown complexion, chiseled frame and long neat dreadlocks may lead one to mistake him for eye

1

candy instead of the rotten apple. It's not just his looks that deceive many, but also his charm and smile that enhance his manipulation skills.

He learned to use that charm to climb the ranks in Newark's Blood Gang organization. His charm coupled with his murder game earned him G status where he comfortably sits near the top of the throne throughout the city. Bugsy made his bones in the streets of Newark when he was barely a teenager. Just a few years over legal age, he's one of the most feared men throughout the entire city.

Most of his life he's been no more than a mere petty nickel and dime hustler with no real success. Anytime that he's been close to success in the drug game, somehow he managed to mess it all up. Whether he blew it by poor decision making or by poor money management, he can never find himself ahead of the game. Opportunity after opportunity he failed, but he refuses to blow this one.

Just a few weeks ago on a humbug he met these Dominican men. After many back and forth conversations, they're finally at a place Bugsy never imagined being at. He knows normally guys of this magnitude wouldn't even entertain him on this level. His charm finally opened the door for a situation that he's sure will change his life forever.

Outlaw Chick

The Dominican in the driver's seat presses the power lock button to secure themselves before the passenger hands the duffle-bag into the backseat to Bugsy who opens the bag anxiously. His adrenaline races as his eyes set on the 10 kilos that are piled up in the bag. He believes now that all of his prayers have been answered. Just as he's about to hand his own duffle-bag over, a white 3 Series BMW bends the corner and stops parallel to them.

The face of a drop dead gorgeous woman snatches the Dominican's attention. With her hand she suggests that the driver roll the window down and he does so without hesitation.

"Can you please tell me how to get to Central Avenue?" she asks in a pleasant tone.

"No speakie Ingles, Mami," the driver replies.

The passenger rises to the edge of his seat. He looks into her eyes charmingly, seeking to attract her. In a fairly decent American dialect he speaks. "Mami, we no from around here. Wait, one second," he says as he turns to look in the backseat. "Central," he manages to utter before staring into the barrel of two chrome semi- automatic handguns.

Bugsy stares down the barrels of the gun that's aimed at the passenger's head, looking coldly into his eyes.

"Don't move! Hands up slow!" he commands.

The driver turns around abruptly and at the sight

3

of the guns, he follows the passenger's lead, raising his hands in the air slowly. Bugsy rests the guns onto their foreheads and with no hesitation he squeezes. The silencers on the guns muffle the sound. The BMW speeds off nervously at the fact of what she just witnessed.

The impact knocks the passenger out of his seat. He lays in a fetal position, curled up under the dashboard while the driver flip flops in his seat. Bugsy lifts up and dumps two shots into the head of the driver. Bugsy coughs violently from the intake of gun smoke that filled the van. Peeking through the thick smoke, he notices that neither of them show any sign of life.

Bugsy peeks around cautiously while tucking his weapons into his waistband. Quickly, he makes his exit out of the van and makes his way to the raggedy Monte Carlo that sits parked waiting for him. He speeds off before he can fully close the door. He speeds down the block before bending a wild right and ripping through the narrow block like a maniac. Through his rearview mirror, he sees a clean getaway. Through his front windshield, he sees promise and a brighter future.

TWO

Bugsy stands in the kitchen of the tidy apartment. In his hands, he holds the most cocaine that he has ever seen with his own eyes. The pure kilo is the most beautiful sight that he's ever laid eyes on, unlike the chalky and compressed product that he's used to handling. He digs into the duffle- bag, just embracing the other nine kilos with joy.

The young woman from the BMW steps into the kitchen, a nervous wreck. She paces around in circles, trying to get herself together. She still can't believe that she allowed herself to be talked into being a part of the entire ordeal. Her first response was refusal but his begging and pleading made her eventually give in. Her love for him forced her to do whatever he asks of her. In the past, he called on her to do a variety of things such as hold drugs for him and even hold guns, but never has he called on her to do anything close to this.

"Are you sure no one saw us?" she asks, seeking his confirmation.

"Who the fuck saw us?" he replies with anger. "Anyway you clear. You didn't do shit! All you did was ask them two dumb motherfuckers for directions! Calm the fuck down!"

"Calm down?" she barks with rage. "Motherfucker, I was just an accomplice to a double homicide," she whispers. "That ain't no normal shit," she says as the tears drip down her face. "I don't know how I even allowed you to talk me into some crazy shit like this," she says as she plants her face into the palms of her hands. "You said nothing about murder."

"In every robbery there's a chance that murder can be the end result. Whether it be the *robbee* or the *robber,* you charge it to the game."

As she stands there, her whole life flashes before her eyes. She realizes her small role in this escapade could get the average person a minimum of fifteen years in prison and she's not even the average person.

"I'm a fucking cop," she whispers. "Did you forget? If anybody ever hears a word of this I'm going to be put under the jail," she cries as she fall to pieces.

Several months ago, she was known to the world as plain old, Shontay. As of two months ago, she's now known as rookie cop, Shontay Baker. Their love affair began long before she even thought of being a cop. Through one of their many breakups, she decided to get on her own feet and stabilize her own future. She took the police exam and to her surprise, she passed with flying colors. Her plan to cut all ties from him and all other street dudes from that point on sounded easier than it actually was. Her obsession for him kept her by his side regardless of the vow that she made to herself. Reality set in that she would never be able to live without him, so she then made other plans for their life together. Foolishly, she thought that she could take care of him, providing all that he needed just to keep him off the streets. She didn't factor in the fact that he loved the streets and his addiction to murder was enough to keep him living a life of crime.

The sound of the ringing doorbell snaps her to. She looks up with fear in her eyes as she stands petrified. Bugsy freezes in mid-motion. The doorbell rings again, this time with more aggression. Shontay stands confused.

Bugsy packs the kilo into the bag and zips it before tiptoeing across the kitchen floor. The doorbell rings again and again. He peeks through the blinds and his freedom flashes before his eyes. Two detectives stand at the door with determination to get inside written all over their faces.

7

Bugsy tiptoes back into the kitchen, staring into Shontay's eyes. The look on his face tells her there's a problem.

"It's the fucking heat," he whispers.

"What?" she asks, going into a nervous frenzy.

"Somebody saw my car. I'm fucked," she cries.

"Calm down. Maybe they ain't here for that. Probably got the wrong house."

"What am I supposed to do?"

He peeks through the side window and sees a clear indication that they don't have the wrong house. One of the detectives is now inside of his car, snooping around. He knows for sure that someone must have seen him. He considers the fact that maybe he was followed here.

"Oh shit, they in my car."

He watches as the detective walks back toward the house. The bell starts ringing again with no pause in between.

"What you want me to do?" she asks desperately.

"Don't answer it."

"Don't answer it? They know we in here. They see the cars out there. Any minute now, they will be busting the doors down."

8

"Hold up," he says as he paces around in circles thinking of a plan. "Let me think a second."

The bell breaks his concentration. He understands that he can't let them bust in on him and catch him with ten kilos and the murder weapons. He has to make a getaway before the whole force arrives.

"Fuck it, answer the door. I'm gone break out through the backdoor."

"But what about me?" she asks, feeling as if he's only thinking of himself.

"They don't have shit on you. It's me they're looking for."

"But your car is in my driveway. They will know that you were here with me."

"They can't prove that shit. Just act like you never seen that car before. Those plates don't come back to nobody. For all they know, somebody just ditched the car in your driveway."

The bell rings continuously and they both realize that they're running out of time.

"Just do what the fuck I say. Answer the door and act like you don't know what they're talking about. You don't know shit about that car. Point blank period," he says as he creeps toward the back door.

Outlaw Chick

Shontay takes a few deep breaths in between the doorbell pauses. She uses slow strides toward the door, preparing her alibi as she walks along. Bugsy grabs the door and takes one long look back at her before opening it. He quickly places one gun into the duffle-bag and holds the other one tight in his grip.

Through the small window, he sees the shock of his lifetime. Another detective stands at the back door.

"Oh, shit," he mumbles to himself as he pictures himself in cuffs being dragged away. With no time to think, he does what he thinks is best. There's only one thing in between him and his freedom and he must remove it.

He grips his gun tighter before snatching the door open. A third detective stands in surprise before reaching for his gun but it's already too late. He's been beaten to the draw. Bugsy aims at his forehead and squeezes.

The detective drops onto his knees before rolling down the steps lifelessly. Bugsy steps over him with a single leap down the small flight of stairs. He hops over the gate in the backyard and stops in his tracks when he thinks of the love of his life that he's left behind to take the weight for his actions. He quickly visions the look of fear that was

10

in her eyes and the only thing he can think of after that is her rolling over and bringing him in. He can't leave her behind if he wishes to pull this caper off. He turns around and climbs back over the gate. He sprints through the alley. Once at the end of the alley, he peeks his head out surveying the area which appears to still be clear. He tiptoes up the stairs and walks through the opened doors.

His heart beat with fear as he sees the back of both of the detective's heads. They stand in front of Shontay who seems to have lost all composure. It's obvious that they will be able to get the absolute truth out of her. She's crying hysterically until she looks up and sees him. Her eyes pop open with suspense.

Before the detectives can look back, Bugsy leaps at them. He bangs the first detective in the back of the head and as he drops, Bugsy already has his gun aimed at the head of the other detective. The detective looks down at his partner who lays dead in a pool of blood and backs up, reaching for his gun nervously. Bugsy darts at him, ramming the gun into the detective's face. He squeezes with vengeance and watches with great satisfaction as the detective falls face first. Gratification fills his eyes as he watches the detective take his last breath before keeling over.

Outlaw Chick

Shontay covers her eyes in an attempt to block out what she just witnessed. Sirens roar in the distance coming from every direction. Bugsy catches Shontay by her hand and runs out of the hallway, dragging her out with him. As they're running toward her car, the sounds of the sirens are getting closer and closer.

THREE

Bugsy zips down the turnpike in deep concentration. He utters the words of Jay-Z and Beyoncé's, *On the Run,* which blasts through the speakers.

"Boy meets girl, girl perfect woman. Girl gets to bustin' before the cops come running!" he shouts animatedly before slamming a palm full of pills into his mouth.

He places the bottle of Codeine syrup up to his mouth, tilts his head back and devours it in one gulp. He slams the bottle to the floor. Despite the focused and certain look in his eyes, he's as confused as he's ever been. He has not a clue of his next destination. As he looks at the red fuel light on the dashboard indicating low fuel, he realizes they won't get far. He holds 10 kilos that will eventually be transformed into currency. He has no doubt about that, but right now his pockets are empty. Shontay's pockets are empty as well due to the fact that she was drug out of the house, no purse, no phone, not even shoes, just bedroom slippers.

13

Shontay sits upright in the passenger's seat in a trance-like state. She stares straight ahead but what plays before her eyes is not the heavy traffic flow before them. What she sees is the series of events that have just taken place. It plays back like a movie. Every few minutes, she closes her eyes and opens them, hoping that all of this this is one big nightmare.

She can't believe that any of this has taken place. She questions herself about how she even allowed herself to be caught up like this. She has already accepted the fact that her life is over. All that she's worked for is gone down the drain, just like that. Her life has been destroyed at the hands of a man. A man that everyone that loves her told her she shouldn't be with. If only she had listened, she wouldn't be in this situation. She closes her eyes once again and her mind goes back to how it all started.

The song that she and Bugsy had their very first dance to plays clearly in her mind. Their bodies glued together as the voice of Drake sings over the Best I Ever Had track. He two-stepped as she controlled the dance floor, making them a spectacle for all to see. He spun her around like a ballerina and placed his forehead against hers. She backed away, dancing seductively in front of him.

Their eyes intertwined, and they stared deep into each other's soul.

The chemistry that she felt was unimaginable. No formal meeting, just two minutes of dancing and she felt as if she'd known him her entire life. Strangely, she felt that this was her soulmate. A few drinks at the bar and not only did they formally introduce themselves, but they got to know each other the best they could over the loud music that blared in their ears. A few more drinks and they were on the dance floor grinding away again.

The night was ending, but neither of them wanted it to. He begged her to stay the night with him and as badly as she wanted to resist, she didn't. Her friends begged her to not go, reminding her that she didn't know him well enough to leave with him. They claimed that she was allowing the alcohol to think for her, but even drunk she knew that the alcohol may have played a small part in it. Their chemistry was her deciding factor. She'd always been a sucker for the bad guy. His bad guy demeanor coupled with his charm had won her over. The lights finally come on in the club and her friends said farewell with nervousness on their faces.

"Don't worry, y'all," she slurred. "I'm a big girl. I can handle myself."

He grabbed her hand and gently pulled her away from them. They both staggered away from the club, using each other to hold themselves up.

In the middle of the block, they put on another show. In front of the many people that were making their way to their cars, they kissed each other passionately like two characters in a Soap Opera series.

"Get a room!" a woman yelled in a teasing manner.

They were oblivious to the laughing and loud cheering. The only thing they could hear was the sound of their beating hearts pounding against each other. Shontay's body heated up making her hotter than she'd ever been. The orgasm that she felt taking place in her panties was one that she'd never felt during actual sexual intercourse and she was amazed that it was happening with no intercourse at all. She was so hot that she would allow him to take her right there in front of everyone and blame it all on the alcohol later.

They continued kissing a few steps until finally he stopped. He pressed her against the back door of a raggedy Jeep Cherokee, and they continued their intense make out session. Before she knew it, the back door was being opened and she was being laid out like a baby onto the backseat. Inside the truck, they made passionate love and indulged in back breaking raunchy sex, all in the same session. Behind the tints, they could not be seen, but the bouncing of the truck caught the attention of all the people in passing. Shontay had never done anything as spontaneous as this and she loved it. Never had she had a man that could bring out the beast in her.

It was that night that she finally understood why good girls love bad guys. Shontay opened her eyes and the beautiful memory washed away. It's not hard to wash away the memory because it was so long ago and the only thing to follow that beautiful night was misery. At times, she felt that he baited her with all the things she yearned and desired, only to give her all the things she never wanted for herself. It seemed as if heartache and pain was all that he was capable of dishing out. She'd accepted the fact that he took great pleasure in hurting people, but that's all he seemed to know. He would bring pain to her and anyone else that got in the way of whatever he wanted.

Their relationship was built on love but revolved around the fear that she had of him. Anytime she'd considered leaving him her fear of what he may do to her changed her mind. He'd even threatened to harm her family members as well. Those threats she'd charge off as his jealousy for her. One thing she knows for certain, his jealousy wasn't to be taken lightly.

She thought back to a time a few years ago. She stood in the cut of a small neighborhood bar. In front of her, stood a young man that she had been pushing away all night. His persistence kept him in the picture.

"I'm not leaving without your number," he said with a dazzling smile.

"I already told you, I have a fiancée," she said in an agitated tone.

She looked over to her best friend and the fearful look that she displayed could only mean one thing. Her friend couldn't muster the words, but she looked over to the doorway where Bugsy stood.

"Go, please just go," she commanded, however, the young man ignored her.

Bugsy approached quickly with rage in his eyes. He stood behind the man who turned around, quite in shock.

Shontay speaks out of fear. "Babe, it's not what it looks like."

"Babe? Nigga all in your face and now I'm babe!"

"I been telling him all night to leave me alone, but he wouldn't."

The young man looked at her with shock. He looked to Bugsy with a cocky look, trying to cover the fear that was in his heart.

"Shit funny to you? You think it's a game?"

Outlaw Chick

"Aye man, this ain't got nothing to do with me. This between you and your lady. Your chick in the spot, niggas gone push," he said with a smirk.

Without warning, Bugsy grabbed the young man by his neck and lifted him off of the ground. The man's eyes bulged out of his head as the life was being choked out of him. Two bouncers come to the young man's rescue. One pried his hands from the man's neck while the other pushed him away. Bugsy lost all composure and commenced to fighting both the bouncers off of him. Singlehandedly, he dominated them until another bouncer came over and evened the score. Together they managed to drag him to the entrance of the bar. Shontay followed behind them, attempting to help them off of her lover.

As he was being pushed out of the door, he stared at the young man with the 1000 yard stare. The only thing in his eyes was war. The young man stared back at him in mockery.

An hour later and Bugsy and Shontay sat in the car directly across from the bar. "Please, can we just go?" she begged from the passenger's seat. "It's not that serious."

"It is that serious. You made it that serious," he says before his attention was captured by the crowd of people who were exiting the bar.

Bugsy snatched both of his weapons from his

waistband. *"Now I'm about to show you how serious shit is."*

Bugsy's eyes were glued to the young man that staggered out of the bar. He rolled down the ski mask that he wore on his head, covering his face entirely.

"Please don't do this!" Shontay cried.

Bugsy bust the door open and stepped into the darkness. People dispersed frantically at the sight of him with the guns in his hands. The fear on the people's faces sped up his adrenaline. His prey stood there, too drunk to move. He stood in fear as Bugsy stepped closer to him. Once within arm's reach of the man, Bugsy squeezed with the gun he held in his right hand. The young man stumbled backwards. As he laid on the ground crawling to save his life, Bugsy fired consecutive shots from both guns until the man was no longer moving. Bugsy raced back to the car, hopped into the seat, and sped off. He looked over to Shontay with a devious smile on his face.

"Thank yourself for what just happened to him. If you wouldn't have been here, this would've never happened."

Although she knew she was totally innocent in the matter, in her heart she felt responsible for the outcome. Because of that incident, she's stayed clear of clubs and anything that could bring out that *jealous streak in him. At times, she felt like a slave to this relationship; but love, fear and stupidity had kept her in it.*

In her heart, she knows that she should have left him long ago but she didn't. She stayed out of love and out of fear. All she wanted was for him to change and give her that feeling that she felt when she first laid eyes on him. Like a crack addict chasing the high he obtained from his first hit, she stayed in the game chasing that hit she never got. And now this. Her high is blown. Her mind now revisits all the pain that she's felt over the past years until her face is soaking wet with tears.

"Oh shit," Bugsy says as he finally breaks his silence.

His words snap her out of the past and bring her into the right now. She looks over to him and sees him pointing at the overhead sign that they're approaching. Shontay's eyes bulge out of her head as she reads the letters and numbers of her license plate on the Alert sign above the highway. She's paralyzed with fear.

Bugsy looks around at the traffic wondering if the people noticed that the car they're reading about is the actual car that's on the road, right beside them. The walls seem to be caving in on them. He realizes they will not be able to get far before the police have them road blocked or boxed in.

"Yo, we gotta get the fuck outta this car. We fucking marked!"

FOUR

Bugsy pulls in to the parking lot of the rest stop. Today must be a busy traveling day because the lot is packed from end to end. He looks around cautiously and so does Shontay. He pulls to the very back of the lot and finds a space in the cut.

"Go ahead," he says as looks over to her. "I will be right here."

She sits in hesitation. "What you gone do, piss on yourself?" he asks enraged. He turns the ignition off in an attempt to save the few drops of gas that's left in the tank.

Shontay opens the door and exits slowly. As she strutted through the lot, she's covered in suspicion. She peeks around nervously. Bugsy waits until she's out of his sight before he loses it for the very first time.

"Fuck!" he shouts as he bangs on the steering wheel.

He bangs his head against the headrest before exhaling all the pity from within. He's been trying to be strong for her. He understands that he can't let

23

her see him fall short. Right now, all her faith is in him and he can't let her see him weak. He has to make her believe that he has a plan, even if he doesn't. He ends the pity party right before Shontay is coming out of the building.

"Think quick, think quick," he mumbles to himself.

Shontay gets in the car and looks over to him for the answers to the problem they have on their hands.

"Now what?"

He ignores her, turning his head away from her as he starts the car. The stalling before starting, tells him that they are now running off fumes. His heart skips a beat but he refuses to let her see him panic. He cruises through the parking lot with his eyes wide open and alert. Suddenly, his attention is caught by tailpipe smoke that's ascending into the air. He tracks the smoke down to a Subaru station wagon that's parked in the center aisle.

She can tell that a bright idea is running through his head. She holds on with desperation, but a part of her fears what he may do next. "What, what are you thinking?" she asks with great curiosity.

He zips over to the Subaru as close as he can get. He peeks through the back window for a sign of a passenger, but he sees none. He looks around and locates an empty space. With no further delay, he backs into it with expertise. He forces the door open.

"Listen, time is everything. When I give you the signal you gotta hurry," he says before getting out of the car.

Shontay sits back, one second away from a nervous breakdown. She watches him closely, wondering what his next move will be and how much more trouble it will get them into. She stares at him without blinking as he tugs the door handle. To his surprise, it opens. He swings the door open and stops dead in his tracks.

Bugsy is in shock at the two children who sit in the backseat. A little girl about the age of eight stares at Bugsy like a deer staring into headlights. She screams at the top of her little lungs. Her scream pierces through the airwaves and awakens the baby that was sleeping in the car seat next to her. Both children are now crying loudly.

Bugsy waves Shontay on. She busts the door open and just as she's about to get out, she thinksof her valuables that are in the car. She fumbles clumsily with the keys before opening the glove compartment. She snatches her gun box with quickness. Her badge falls onto the floor. She quickly retrieves the badge, slams the compartment shut and makes her exit. She slams the door and runs over to the Subaru.

"Shhh," Bugsy says to the little girl as he unstraps the car seat from under the seatbelt. The little girl screams that much louder. He pulls her by her hand, yanking her out of the car. Shontay stands there with sympathy in her eyes as she stares at the crying helpless babies.

"Get in!" he commands as he pulls the little girl to the front of the car.

He plants the car-seat on the ground gently and runs to the car. He gets in the driver's seat and backs out of the parking spot as inconspicuously as he can.

"Adding car theft to our list of charges, huh?" she says in sarcasm.

"Right now they're looking for *us* for five murders, this car theft shit is a misdemeanor. Trust me," he says as he cruises the lot slowly until he hits the turnpike ramp.

He then steps on the gas as he pushes the car as fast as it can go. She has not a reply for him. She just sits back in disbelief as she stares at the badge that she holds in her hand. The tears well up before soaking her face. Just a few hours ago, life was as normal as could be. She looks at the badge through teary eyes and accepts the fact that life as she knew it is no longer.

FIVE

Shontay lays back in the passenger's seat asleep. She cried herself to sleep minutes ago. Her eyes pop open groggily. She peeks over to Bugsy, looks at the dashboard and reading the word *Subaru*, reminds her that this is reality and not a nightmare. She looks over to Bugsy with disgust as she now hates him for dragging her into this. Foolishly, she had hoped she could fall asleep and awaken like none of this had happened.

She snaps out of her grogginess as her eyes brush across the billboard over the turnpike. Her picture under the word *WANTED* causes her heart to stop beating. She can't utter a word, so she points at the sign. Bugsy looks up in even more shock than her as he reads the words under her picture aloud.

"Police Officer Shontay Baker wanted in connection to five murders. Three of the murders are of Newark City Police Detectives. She's accompanied by an unidentified accomplice. Both are armed and dangerous."

"Shit just got real, Sha," he says staring into her

28

eyes while pausing for seconds. "You ain't a cop no more," he says, seeing the evident sadness. "They just threw you on the opposite side of the fence. You a criminal like me."

"Armed and dangerous," she utters to herself as she stares at the gun box.

She pops the top open, looking at the fully loaded Glock .40. Just to think, yesterday this gun was her weapon that she was given to serve and protect the innocent throughout the city. Today, this same weapon makes her armed and dangerous. She grabs the gun from the box and tucks it in her waistband, not in a holster like a cop, but down her pants like the criminal that they are making her out to be.

One Hour Later...

Bugsy cruises through the run-down streets of North Philly. Shontay stares around observing her surroundings. A long way away from home but somehow she feels a sense of familiarity. The city seems to beat at the same pulse as their own. Being out of Jersey gives her a false sense of comfort. It feels as if she has gotten away from her problems back at home.

Bugsy parks in front of a beat up shack of a house which if not for the lights being on, one would think it was abandoned.

"Now, listen when we get in here keep your composure. Don't even speak even if spoken to. This my blood cousin in here, but I don't trust his ass one bit so neither should you. For that bread, he will flip on his own mother. I'm gone see if I can dump some of this work here to get us some money to keep it pushing. You got me?"

"Yes," she replies as she exhales a deep breath of fear.

He gets out and makes his way to the front door as she tails closely behind. Before they even get to the porch, the front door opens wildly.

Chuck stands in the doorway, arms wide open. "Cuz, what's up? What brings you down here with no warning?"

Another man steps behind him in the doorway. They shake hands and hug at the door as Chuck and the other man looks Shontay up and down with perversion in their eyes.

"And who is this eye candy that you got with you?"

Bugsy stares at the both of them with fire in his eyes. "Nigga, this ain't one of them rats. This my wife right here. Cut the shit."

They see the seriousness in his eyes and immediately remove their eyes from her. Chuck closes the door behind them. "What's the deal though? Everything alright?"

A fake smile covers Bugsy's face. "Everything more than alright. That's why I'm here," he says as he looks over to the man with a look of discomfort on his face.

The look alone forces the man to excuse himself.

"Cuz listen, I ain't got a lotta time. I'm on the bounce. I got a brick of soft in the car and I need to off it."

"A whole brick?" he asks with surprise.

"How much a gram?"

"A gram? Fuck a gram Cuz. I'm trying to get rid of it a one shot deal."

"Nigga, a one shot deal? This ain't the nineties, Cuz. Ain't nobody got no whole brick money," he says with a smile.

"Fuck it, a half, even a quarter but that's it. I ain't trying to be down here camping. I gots to be out."

"What's the rush though, Cuz? What you on the run or something?"

"When you ever known me to run from anything?"

"Well, if that's the case why don't you put your feet up and bust that brick down in small pieces. I can get on the phone and make a few calls and I'm sure I can get through it. Nigga grams equal ounces. The smaller the order the more we can get for it. You know the game."

"Cuz, I ain't got time for all that. Get on your phone and line them niggas up. See if you can reach out to two or three of these niggas that can get together and buy the whole thing. I'm letting it go for dirt cheap."

"What's dirt cheap?"

"The price across the land is 40-43 a bird. All I want is 25 stacks."

Chuck's eyes bulge from his head. "Twenty-five? So you telling me anything over twenty-five is mines?"

"Exactly," Bugsy replies.

"Nigga, come in," Chuck says as he shoves the both of them through the hall. "Have a seat. Let me get on this phone and get this shit popping!"

Three Hours Later...

Shontay lies curled up on the old, worn out couch in comfort as she catches a few ZZZ's. Normally, she wouldn't even stand next to a dirty couch like this, but today she has way more

32

problems than this couch could possibly bring. She's slept through several drug transactions without cracking her eyes not a single time. Chuck sits on the edge of the recliner, counting a stack of unorganized money.

"This another six hundred," he says with pride.

Bugsy stares at him with agitation on his face. "Eight motherfuckers came in here and together all they came up with is seventeen punk ass hundred dollars. Even at the super low they couldn't put no buy money together."

"Cuz, this all was on the spur of the moment."

"Man, fuck that. You need some new friends because the ones you got ain't about shit," he says as he paces around, thinking of his next move.

"I ain't no coke dealer anyway. You know that. I'm a gun merchant," he says in his defense.

A bright idea pops into Bugsy's mind. "You got guns?" he asks quickly.

"Nah, not...not right now," Chuck stutters. "I been waiting for a shipment for a few weeks."

Bugsy shakes his head with a smirk of aggravation.

"What good are you?"

Chuck sits back with no words to reply.

"Can you at least get me some bullets?"

"Oh, I got bullets for days. What you need?"

"I need all the nine millimeter bullets you got."

Shontay's sudden movements snatch his attention away. Her jolting and moaning indicates that she must be having a nightmare. "No!" she cries. "Please, no!"

He runs over and shakes her gently to awaken her. Her body movements has ruffled her clothes, exposing her gun in her waistband. Her eyes pop open with terror in them. He strokes her hair to bring her comfort.

"And I'm gon' need some .40 bullets too," he says as he smoothes her shirt over her gun.

Bugsy paces in silence for minutes before finally saying another word. "Dig, that hooptie you got out there, I'm gonna need it," he says as he points out of the window at the beat up Buick Lacrosse. I need a wheel."

"You need my car? You tripping."

"Listen, I will make it worth your while. Give me your car and I will leave the rest of that bird with you. Go ahead and sell it, score your points off it and give me the rest of my bread," he says with a stern look in his eyes.

Chuck thinks it over for a few seconds before handing over his keys. "You got a deal."

34

"Listen Chuck I don't want no bullshit from you," he says as he sorts through the bag of bullets that lie on the table in front of him. He separates the nine bullets from the .40 bullets. "Don't make me come looking for you. When I call for that bread I need it to be here or we gonna have problems, cut and dry, straight like that. Cousin or no cousin, I need my bread."

"I got you, I got you Cuz. No bullshit, straight up business. When you coming back for the bread though? How long I got?"

"I don't know when I'm coming back," he says as he stands up. He places his bag of bullets into his pocket. "I'm about to hit the road."

Shontay stands up following his lead. They slowly make their way toward the door.

"Hit the road to where?" he interrupts.

"I don't know exactly but when I get to where I'm getting, I'm gon' send for you and my bread. That car I came in," he says pointing to the Subaru through the window. "I need you to get rid of that. It's on fire! Burn that bitch up or something. And whatever you do don't let nobody know I was even here. Nobody," he repeats with emphasis.

Chuck sits back absorbing his cousin's words in silence while many thoughts race through his mind. He doesn't know what's going on, but he knows it must be serious. As curious as he is, he refrains from digging into it. "Cuz, I don't know what you got going on but I'm with you. Just call me and I will be there, you already know."

"I'm gon' call you on that. Once I get to my set location, I will hit you. I'm gone need you to watch my back. I got some big shit in the making." he hands over the big bag of bullets to Shontay. "Here."

Shontay stares at the bullets with confusion. "What's this for?" she mumbles.

"For the .40, just in case.

Shontay shakes her from side to side with sorrow in her eyes. As much as she hates to believe it, she now realizes that she's all the way in and there's no turning back now.

"We out! 'Bout to jump on this highway. Cuz, when I call for you, be on point."

"I will be waiting for your call."

SIX

Bugsy dozed off in the passenger's seat into a deep syrup and pill nod. He was so high he could barely keep his eyes open. He'd been nodding, mouth dragging like a junkie for the past hour as a result of his excessive drug usage. He'd been dumping pill after pill just to clear his mind, but indeed he'd made it fuzzier.

After two near car crashes on the highway, Shontay ordered him to get from behind the wheel. Although she had no clue of where they were going, she felt she had no choice but to take over the wheel. She accepted the fact that eventually, they both would have to face the police that were on heavy on their heels but if taking the wheel could buy them some more time, it was worth the try.

Shontay is so caught up in thought as she's driving, that she doesn't even realize that she's exceeding the Delaware speed limit by over fifteen miles per hour. She doesn't realize it until she spots the Delaware squad car sitting ahead of them in

38

the cut about a half a mile away. As a normal reaction, she hit the brake pedal and decreases the speed abruptly. The jerking of the car snaps Bugsy out of his nod. He looks over to her with anger on his face from blowing his high.

She soars past the squad car at a moderate speed. She peeks in her rearview mirror and the nose of the car seeping out of the cut brings her great alarm. The squad car turns on to the road and cruises the highway. Her heart beat picks up as the speed of the squad car increases. She becomes even more nervous when the car creeps over into the middle lane behind her. Not paying attention to the cars in front of her, she keeps her eyes glued to the rearview mirror.

"He came out!"

"Who came out?" he asks in a slow dragging voice.

"That Delaware cop," she shouts. "I didn't see him in the cut. I was flying. He must have tracked my speed," she says frantically.

Bugsy peeks at the side mirror and seeing the squad car behind them snaps him out of his high. "What the fuck is you stupid? Why the fuck you speeding any fucking way bringing attention to us. You do some dumb ass shit sometimes, I swear! So fucking smart you stupid! I knew I shouldn't have gave your non-driving ass the wheel."

The car speeds up behind them before the lights flash on. A tear of fear drips down Shontay's face. "We fucked!" she shouts.

"Yo, calm the fuck down!"

"Calm down? How you expect me to calm down!"

"Yo, you better calm your stupid ass down!" he says peeking into the mirror. The car comes closer to them, almost banging their bumper.

"He pulling us over. What to do?" she asks in desperation.

"You can't pull the fuck over. That's what the fuck you can't do! You gon' have to take the chase."

"Take the chase?" she shouts in a high pitched tone right before losing it. "Babe, if I don't pull over they're going to box us in any minute. I can't take the chase, I will kill us both in here."

"If you don't take the chase, we both going to jail for fucking ever so we may as well be dead. Now punch that motherfucking gas pedal now! You wanna go to jail forever? Huh?"

"No," she whines.

"Well step on that fucking gas pedal then!"

"I can't," she cries. "I can't."

The sirens stops roaring. "Pull over!" the cop says over the intercom.

"He said pull over," she cries in a panic.

"Bitch, I heard him! But you heard what the fuck I said! Step on it! Five murders, 9 kilos and guns. Ain't no coming back from that. You better take the fucking chase," he barks with aggression.

The cop gently taps the bumper of the car and keeps his bumper glued to them, gently pushing them. Shontay panics and before she even realizes it, she's veering over on the road. She stares at him in shock, not even believing that she pulled over.

Bugsy loses it. "The fuck you doing? You dumb as shit! I should blow your fucking brains out, now we going to jail!" he says as he grabs his gun from under his thigh and grips it tightly. For a second, he actually thinks of carrying out the act but his love for her wipes the thought from his mind. As he stares into the face of the cop sitting in the car behind him through the rearview, another thought quickly comes to mind. He feels as if he has no choice. He grips his gun even tighter as he conceals it against the side of the seat.

The driver's door of the cop car swings open and the tall redneck steps out, looking over his shoulder at the oncoming traffic flow. The closer he gets to the car, the tighter Bugsy grips his weapon. In his mind, he can actually envision the murder that's about to take place. Shontay looks over and she recognizes the look in his eyes that she's seen so many times before.

"Please, no! We already in enough trouble already."

"Sha, it ain't no looking back now. We're all the way in. Just distract him and I will take it from there. We have no choice."

The cop steps to the window, hand on his gun which is still in the holster. He taps the window with aggression. "Roll the window down and turn the ignition off!"

Shontay looks around for the window button before fumbling with it nervously. The cop stares at her with a cherry red face. His eyes are arctic.

"What, y'all don't stop for cops in Pennsylvania?" he asks with sarcasm.

The both of them are confused about the Pennsylvania remark until they realize that he's referring to their license plates.

Bugsy tries to play it cool and not attract any attention to himself. He stares through his peripheral at the cop as he strategizes about the perfect time to make his move.

"I'm sorry Sir," Shontay says in the most innocent tone she could muster under the circumstances. She looks up at him with sad and scared puppy dog eyes. Quickly, she thinks of ways to get her out of this situation. She knows everything depends on it. As an officer, she understands the best way to be with an officer is to be straight up because they all hate bullshit. She also understands that all police love submission. She decides to use all she knows to her advantage. Bugsy already has his mind made up. He's sure the cop will eventually stick his head in the window and when he does, he plans to blow his head off of his shoulders.

"License, insurance," he says as he slowly kneels down, preparing to stick his head in the window. Bugsy's mental alarm goes off, signaling that it's show-time. He gently taps the trigger as he wraps his hand tightly around the handle. Still, he keeps his eyes glued to the windshield.

The cop begins to lower his head into the car. With his left hand, Bugsy reaches upward as if he's about to retrieve the paperwork, only to buy himself some time.

Shontay's watches Bugsy with fear and suspense. She realizes she has to say something quick.

"Officer, I apologize for my speeding. I didn't realize I was going that fast until it was too late and I didn't want to further disrespect you by slowing down like that."

A sudden look at the middle console sparks a light in the cop's eyes. "What's that?" he asks pointing.

Both Bugsy and Shontay see the badge in clear view. Their hearts stop beating at the same time.

"Let me see that," he demands with his hand inside the car.

Shontay looks over to Bugsy with fear in her eyes before reaching slowly for her badge. She hands it to him and lowers her head in sadness. She realizes that her life is over at this point.

The cop snatches the badge and read the name on it. He pauses for seconds.

Now! the voice in Bugsy's head shouts out. He peeks over into the cop's face for the very first time. He slowly slides his gun from underneath his thigh. He gauges the distance in between him and the cop. He prays that he can hit him with one fatal shot because missing will bring all types of other problems. He studies his mark, focusing on the spot right in between his eyes.

"Who is Baker?"

"Me," Shontay mumbles.

"New Jersey cop?" he asks.

It takes everything in her to keep a straight face on, without falling apart in fear. She nods her head up and down without the ability to utter a single word. Bugsy now has his gun positioned for his draw.

"You're a long way away from home, huh?" He

stares at her in silence for three long seconds. "You know better than speeding on my highway. This ain't New Jersey," he says sarcastically. Bugsy holds the gun at his waist side. "I'm going to give you a pass today," he says as he hands the badge back into the window.

Shontay looks into his eyes with surprise on her face. Bugsy looks into his eyes as well, not knowing if he should blow his brains out or just hold out to see how it will play out. He decides on the latter.

"You remember this and make sure you tell all your Jersey cops that I let you live. Any of us come through your state, I expect the same treatment. Deal?"

Shontay replies with hesitation. "Yes, deal," she says with gratitude in her eyes. Neither of them actually believe the words that he's said until his cop stature becomes at ease and he takes a step away from the car. "Have a good day and take it easy in my state. The next cop may not be as flexible as me."

Bugsy eases the grip off his gun and slowly he lets his hand drop against the seat.

"Thank you kind Sir," Shontay says graciously.

The cop salutes her before turning about face and walking toward his car. Shontay looks over at Bugsy with tears of joy in her eyes.

"Yo, go before he change his fucking mind and

go back there running a name check." She twists the key in the ignition and cruises off at a respectful speed. The cop car speeds past them with his sirens roaring. They both exhaled deeply, thanking God.

SEVEN

Bugsy sits on the edge of the worn out bed here in the Motel 6. The extremely close call has shaken them both up. They both agreed that they should take it as a warning and not push their luck. They decided that they should check in and get some sleep so they can collect their thoughts and plan the next move but Shontay has made it impossible for him to even think.

He looks up with anger and frustration. "Will you please! I can't even hear myself think! You're fucking killing me!"

"I'm killing you? Motherfucker, fuck you! We are in this mess because of you," she cries. "Now we in the middle of fucking nowhere on the fucking run!" she shouts.

Bugsy looks around with paranoia in his eyes as he rushes her and places his hand over her mouth.

"Yo, shut the fuck up," he whispers. "You trying to get us fucking caught?"

She wiggles from his grip but he manages to keep his hand cupped over mouth. That is, until she bites down

48

on the palm of his hand until she tastes his blood. He snatches his hand from her mouth and pushes her with all of her might.

"Bitch!"

Shontay stares at him with a look in her eyes that he's never seen. Like a vicious pit bull, she leaps at him, almost knocking him off his feet.

"You ruined my fucking life," she cries. "You fucking bastard," she says as she slaps him with all of her might causing his neck to snap. He becomes furious but he keeps his cool and just allows her to vent and pour out her frustration. She kicks, punches and scratches him but really brings him no pain.

He grabs her by her shoulder and restrains her. "Sha, stop, please?" he begs.

Holding her only infuriates her more. With total disrespect, she spits in his face. Bugsy stands in shock, not believing that she's done this. Before he knows it, she's laying on her back on the bed from the brutal slap he's just given her. He straddles himself over, preparing to finish her off. Right before he drops his fist onto the center of her pretty little face, he catches himself.

He palm grips her face, squeezing the life out of it. "Bitch, if you ever disrespect me like that, I will beat the shit outta you."

49

She stares into his eyes with fear. Seeing her afraid like this melts his heart. He now becomes saddened that he's even laid hands on her.

He gets off of her and plops onto the bed next to her. She sobs loudly as the reality of this all sinksin. For the first time since all of this began, she hasn't had a moment to think due to everything happening so fast. As she replays it all and visualizes her picture on the billboard, her sobbing gets louder. "I fucking hate you!"

He snatches her from the bed and hugs her tightly. "Sha, I'm sorry. I didn't mean for any of this to happen. I got you in this mess and I will get you out of it. I promise you. Just give me a minute to think and I will come up with a plan," he says as he lifts her face from his chest. He stares into her flooded eyes and tears begin to drip from his own eyes.

"Please baby, just work with me. I will come up with a plan that will get you out of this. That's my word."

EIGHT

Two Hours Later...

Bugsy dragged her out of the motel room and they ended up here in this small local strip bar, not too far away. She wanted to stay back at the hotel, but for some reason he didn't trust her alone. The way she performed earlier made him not trust her. A part of him now looks at her as if she's against him. Before all of this, he would trust her with his life, but now with the rage and the hate she expressed, the tables have turned.

The strip bar is quite different from what both of them know strip joints to be. A bunch of skinny white Russian women prancing across the stage with no rhythm. The music is quite unfamiliar to them. They watch as white businessmen place the money in the women's hands respectfully, unlike the groping of the women that they're used to seeing.

Shontay sits away from him with a coldness that freezes the room. Just as the barmaid slides a second round of Ciroc over the bar to them, a white man parks a seat right next to Bugsy. He looks over with anger as the man who is obviously drunk, bumps shoulders with him. He sees the look on Bugsy's face.

"You alright?" he asks with arrogance on his face.

Bugsy ignores him by looking away from him. Shontay moves closer and nudges him with her arm as a signal to calm down.

"If you alright, I'm alright," the man says as he shouts to the barmaid. "My whistle is dry over here! What the fuck?"

The barmaid races over with a drink in her hand. She hands it to him staring submissively into his eyes. "And don't let my glass go empty or I will have your job."

The woman nods her head in a bow as she steps away from him. The man stares at his phone reading the display through one half closed drunken eye. He then slams the phone onto the bar almost knocking Bugsy's drink over.

Bugsy looks over at him with rage in his eyes. The man looks back at him with no regard to his rage.

"You wanna use my phone?" he the man asks.

"What?" Bugsy asks with fury bleeding from his lips.

"I said, do you want to use my phone?"

"Use your phone for what? I got my own fucking phone."

"Okay," he says as he looks away. He looks back staring into Bugsy's eyes as he slams the phone back on to the bar. "I asked you do you want to use it. Now if you steal it, I will have your head"

Bugsy is in shock at his courage and finds it quite humorous for the most part. "Have my head?" he asks with a smirk.

"You don't know me?" he asks. "Better ask somebody in this bar. I run this city. I'm a big deal."

"I don't care to know you. Just drink your drink and leave me the fuck alone. I'm begging you."

Bugsy and Shontay sip away in silence as the strippers come over to the man one by one. They treat him like royalty and he treats them like servants.

After three back to back drinks, the man slides his chair away from the bar and gets up staggering. "You see my drink, my wallet and my phone right there?" he asks as he rocks back and forth.

Bugsy fights every urge to get up and bang the man's head onto the bar. He just looks away from the man as if he isn't standing there. "When I come back it all better still be here," he says as he staggers away.

"Babe, let's go," Shontay begs as a precaution to what she sees is inevitable to happen.

"Nah, fuck that! Fuck him! We ain't going nowhere."

Another man quickly steps to Bugsy's side. He stands behind the chair. Bugsy peeks over his shoulder at the man with discomfort in his eyes. "What? What the fuck you want?"

The man leans over to whisper to Bugsy. "Hey man don't mind him. "He's an obnoxious asshole. His name is Jack and everybody in the bar hates him but no one has the heart to stand up to him. We just ignore him."

"I ain't everybody, I'm me," Bugsy says as he looks away.

"He runs this city and can bring big problems and make it hard to live here."

"Well, I don't live here so fuck him."

"He's connected."

"Connected to who? I don't give a flying fuck."

"He's connected to the Russian Mob. He's something like a Don. He's not a Don but he's affiliated. He has them in his pocket and they will do anything that he tells them to do."

The man comes staggering out of the bathroom and the over-friendly stranger stops talking. He quickly makes his way back to his seat. The drunkard man takes his seat. He starts back at Bugsy immediately. "Everything still here. That's a good thing, for your sake," he says before taking a huge gulp of his drink.

Bugsy's attention is captured by the white powder residue which coats the tip of his nose. That residue brings all types of thoughts into his mind. Bugsy looks at him and wipes his own nose signaling the man to wipe his nose and he does.

"Just a little coke," he says with no shame. "Everybody does a little coke don't they?"

For the first time Bugsy cracks a smile at the man. "I guess so."

The man extends his hand over to Bugsy with a bill in his grip. "Here, have some." Bugsy doesn't budge. "Here take it. It's rude to tell me no. Here."

"I'm good but thanks. I got my own."

"You don't have what I got. A nigger like you can't get your hands on the quality of powder I can get. This ain't that cut up cheap quality they have in your little nigger ghetto hood. Try it and you will thank me later."

Bugsy disregards all his racial remarks for he's now thinking business. He digs into his pocket and retrieves a small baggy filled with about a gram or two. He hands it over to the man discreetly. The man looks at his hand before reaching for it.

Bugsy gets up from his seat and Shontay follows. "When I come back here, you tell me what you think about it."

The man looks at the bag in his hand and the crystals from the cocaine sparkled through the darkness like a disco ball. His adrenaline begins to race just looking at it. He places the bag up to his nose and takes a whiff. The pungent odor of the pure cocaine rips through the plastic. He quickly begins to untie the bag as Bugsy is stepping away.

"Wait a minute, please. Give me a phone number so I can find you if I like it," he says with no doubt in his mind that he will like it. He can spot quality cocaine from miles away and he's sure that this is it. "How will I be able to find you?"

Bugsy continues to step away. He stops short. "Don't try to find me. I will find you."

NINE

Two Days Later...

Jack closes the door of his spacious office for privacy. The hustle and bustle of his Import/Export company takes place all throughout the five story building. Shipping products, such as vehicles, food, clothing and even illegal products to and from Russia provides a lavish lifestyle. This business is the bridge between him and the Russian Mafia. Shipping their drugs and guns through his company makes him a valuable asset to them.

Jack makes his way over to his desk where Bugsy is already unwrapping the rubber casing that covers the kilo. Jack watches with anxiety while Shontay sits in the far corner of the room out of the way. Last night, Bugsy found Jack in the same bar they met in the night before, just like he said he would. Unlike their initial meeting, Jack was very inviting.

Jack rolled out the red carpet for Bugsy and had drinks poured for him and Shontay all night long, all compliments of him. He was like a totally different person. Instead of treating them like lower class citizens, he treated them like royalty. As a businessman, he knows how to play the game to get what he wants and what he wants is the cocaine that Bugsy gave him a sample of.

Shontay is against Bugsy doing business with him. She doesn't trust him at all. Bugsy doesn't trust him either, but he realizes he must put his trust in someone in order to get his product moved. He's been taking risks all his life for smaller money with real killers, so he looks at this as nothing. He also believes this deal can bring him no more trouble than he is already in.

Bugsy hands the half opened kilo over to Jack as Jack takes a seat behind his desk. His eyes never leave the brick. "So, this is the exact same product you had in the little baggie that night? Don't come at me with the old bait and switch."

Jack stares at the sparkling white cocaine and his question is answered. He licks his lips with greed in his eyes. He looks up for the very first time since he touched the work.

"Let me ask you, how does a little poor black kid like yourself get your hands on such high quality product?"

"Let's just say that you're not the only one that's connected," he replies with a straight face. "I told you that work you get ain't on the level of mines. Let me school you on something. You white boys up on the high horse think you so smart but you're stupid. The grade A work is in the ghetto nigger hoods as you call it. That shit y'all get is stepped on and cut up and y'all dummies pay top dollar for it," he says with a smile.

"You think?" Jack asks with a smirk. "You may be on to something. So, let me ask you what will work of this quality cost me?"

Bugsy thinks hard on the right price to charge him. He has no idea what Jack is used to paying. He doesn't want to shortchange himself knowing that he has Jack exactly where he wants him. The going rate in the hood is mid-forties per gram but he understands that he's not in the hood. He's dealing with a more prestigious clientele and he can get top dollar. Jack sprinkles a little powder onto the edge of his desk. He interrupts Bugsy's thought process by speaking again.

"Aye girl, fetch me that straw on the windowsill behind you," he says to Shontay in a commanding voice. Shontay looks at him with disgust before rolling her eyes away from him as if he hasn't said a word.

"Girl, what's the matter you deaf or dumb?" he asks as Shontay looks over to Bugsy with fiery eyes.

"What's the matter with your bitch? She don't follow instructions? Bitches are like dogs," he says staring through her with disgust. "You gotta train them."

"Not your instructions. She follows my instructions and my instructions only. Second of all, she ain't my bitch. She ain't no girl to you, and she ain't here to fetch shit," Bugsy says as he steps around the desk and stands over Jack.

For the very first time, Jack shows fear. Bugsy points in his face, tip of finger against Jack's nose with disrespect. "If you ever disrespect her again, I will murder you and wait for the repercussions," he says as he lifts his shirt, exposing the guns that are tucked in his waistband. Jack stares at the guns as he swallows a lump of fear in his throat.

"You got everybody else walking on eggshells but not me. I don't give a fuck about you or no Russian Mafia. If you ever disrespect me or mines in any form it will take the whole Russian army to take me down," he says while tapping Jack's nose with each syllable. "I let you get away with that drunk shit the other night. I see how you talk to everybody else but I ain't everybody else. You gon' respect me. You understand me?"

Jack subdues to the ultimate form of submission. "Yes, understood," he says lowering his eyes onto his desk.

"Good that we have that clear. Now apologize to her," he demands.

He looks over to Shontay with hatred on his face. It goes against everything that he believes, but still he does it. "I apologize," he mumbles.

"Now back to business," Bugsy says. "I got a special price for you. I'm gone need fifty-five thousand for that."

"Fifty-five? I don't pay a dollar over forty grand for product."

"But you said it yourself you don't get this quality of work. Haven't had it like this in years. You can keep buying that cut up garbage or you can get the good shit. It's up to you. We got a deal or what?"

Jack wants to put up a fight but the longer the fight he puts up the longer it will take for him to bury his nose into the cocaine. "Deal!"

TEN

Days Later...

A slightly drunken Bugsy sits in the strip bar in his rightful seat. In the few short days, he and Shontay has become regulars at the bar. Not only are they regulars, they are amongst the most important people group in the bar. They're treated like celebrities due to the fact of how Jack has laid everything out for them making them as comfortable as he possibly can. The way he caters to them gives everyone no other choice but to cater to them in the same manner. They've hardly ever seen him respect anyone like he respects Bugsy and that calls for a great deal of respect from them.

Bugsy now has Jack in his pocket in a way that he hadn't expected. Any request he has, Jack brings it to life. Jack will do anything to keep their line of business open. He rented a 5 star hotel suite for them in his name, and got them out of the uncomfortable Motel 6.

Jack also introduced him to more clients. A few of them are big spenders but none are of the same magnitude of him. Bugsy is grateful for all business because the money still adds up, even if it's a few hundred bucks at a time. Jack even introduced him to his flunky, Pepe. Jack informed him that Pepe is loyal, hardworking and most of all trustworthy. He suggested that he use him as his fall guy just to keep him safe and sound and keep his hands clean. His goal is to keep Bugsy protected and comfortable so he can always have access to the work that he has fallen in lust with.

Bugsy's fall guy Pepe is loaded up every day with 8-Balls, measured out exactly at 3.5 grams that he distributes to customers as well as dancers who indulge. At a hundred dollars per gram, the 8-Balls value at $350. Pepe is paid $70 an 8-Ball. At a minimum of approximately 20, 8-Balls a day, they've been grossing about $7,000 a night.

He had no expectations that he would acquire this type of business in such a short time. Even back at home he's never made seven grand a day in all his years of hustling. Foolishly, he's convinced himself that maybe all of this happened for a reason because under no other circumstances would he ever have come here. Now that he's finally found success, he has no plans of ever leaving here. He's made himself quite at home and the money has helped him to forget all about the trouble that awaits him at home.

Pepe makes his way over to Bugsy where he takes a seat right next to him. Under the bar, he hands Bugsy a hefty stack of money.

"That's three grand right there."

Bugsy takes the money and quickly tucks it into his jacket pocket while staring at the doorway wherein Shontay walks into the bar with an armful of shopping bags.

She's been in a deep depression and he hates to see her like this. He knows how much she loves to shop, so that's the only thing he knows to do for her to cheer her up. Each morning before he leaves for the bar, he gives her a few dollars to shop her depression away. The $5,000 that she's blown through so far, would've meant a great deal to her under normal conditions, but truly means nothing at all now. The shopping keeps her mind occupied, but she can't help but to be reminded of all that's going on right now.

Shontay comes over to Bugsy and hugs him with a look of misery covering her face. "Hey," she whispers before giving him a rather dry peck on his lips.

Seeing her like this breaks his heart but there's nothing he can do to take it all back now. None of this was in his plans so he has to just take it how it comes. He's more worried about her than he is himself. He knows he can handle anything that comes out of it but his concern is her. The fact that he's ruined her whole life breaks his cold heart into pieces.

"Come on babe, cheer up," he whispers in her ear accompanied by a tight comforting hug.

Pepe quickly gets out of her seat and takes position behind Bugsy. Bugsy loos at the barmaid who stands before them. "Give her a triple of her regular."

Pepe leans close enough to whisper in Bugsy's ear. "My friend I told you about is here," he says as he nods toward the opposite end of the bar.

"Pepe, I told you I really don't want to meet nobody. Any business he wants to do can come through you."

"But he's good. I would like y'all to meet. Please just trust me on this one. He makes big moves."

Bugsy sighs with agitation. "Okay, for you Pepe. Anything goes wrong me and you got problems."

"There will be no problems. I've known him for years." Pepe gives a head nod and a short Spanish dude begins to make his way around the bar.

Bugsy watches him closely trying to get a read on him. It's not that he's really against meeting new people. It's just that he's found comfort in this situation. He's never made money this easy in all of his life and he's quite content with the way things are going. At the rate that he's going, it may take him months to finish the 8 kilos that he has left but at least he will be able to do it with very minimal risk.

It's hard for him to read the man due to the blank look on his face and his low key demeanor. He appears to be the common Mexican standing, at the 'Work for Hire' spots. The closer he gets to him, he can read sincerity and honesty in his eyes. He stands before Bugsy with a humbling demeanor. He bows his head down before staring square into Bugsy's eyes.

"Mike," Pepe says addressing Bugsy by his alias. "This is my good friend Domingo. Domingo, this is Mike." They shake hands tightly, staring into each other's eyes.

"So, what's up?" Bugsy asks before taking a swig of his drink.

In a shaky voice, Domingo begins to speak. "My good friend, he tell me all about you and your business you got going. I got my hands on a little of the work and move it with my customers. They love it. It move too fast though. Not enough money to buy the amount I really need, you know?"

Bugsy brushes him off rather arrogantly. "But what you trying to say though?"

Domingo swallows the lump in his throat before speaking again. "I know you don't know me, but if you could let me get a little on consignment I can make big things happen."

Bugsy interrupts hastily. "I don't do consignment. Money on the wood," he says as he bangs onto the bar.

"Listen, I can make it worth your while. I will bring you in 50/50. Listen before I go away I had big business. Maybe 30 to 40 kilos a week. I do five years and come home to nothing. All my peoples away."

Bugsy stares at him in shock. He's still stuck at the 30-40 kilos a week. All he has is 8 so he estimates them being done in a couple of days. He can envision himself standing over close to a half of million in cash. That would be a dream come true for him. He figures that's more than enough money for him and Shontay to go far away from here and live happily ever after.

Domingo continues on with his business pitch. "Give me maybe a half a kilo and we go down the middle. I'm not greedy. A half a kilo of soft, I whip into a whole thing. Give you your price and everything else we split. We can take over all of Wilmington and Dover Downs easy. This little money here in the bar is nothing compared to the money flowing through all of Delaware."

Domingo now has his full attention. "Is that so? You talking a good game."

"It's not talk. All I need is a chance and I can back up everything I say."

Bugsy looks over to Pepe. "You vouch for him right?"

"A hundred percent," Pepe replies.

"Okay, I will give him a shot but I already told you anything goes wrong, and you got big problems," Bugsy says with sincerity in his eyes. "I don't get my money back or any problems, both of you will be held accountable," he says in a threatening manner.

Bugsy's looks away for a second just to take account of his surroundings. His eyes roll pass the huge big screen that's posted on the wall and by pure coincidence, what is on the screen causes his face to drop in surprise. The clear picture of Shontay on the screen sobers him quickly.

The words 'WANTED IN NEW JERSEY' is printed boldly across the bottom of the screen. He quickly peeks over to Shontay who is already staring at the screen. She's petrified, not able to move, not even a facial muscle. Once she's able to move, she ducks her head low with her hand covering her face hoping that no one notices that it's her on the screen.

Bugsy quickly tries to distract Pepe and Domingo to keep their attention from the screen. "Listen, we get together tomorrow and we make some things happen," he says as he peeks around the bar to see if anyone is paying attention to the TV. They all seem to be drunk and not paying any attention. He nudges Shontay with his arm and signals her to exit the bar.

Her sudden movement causes them concern. They both look at her with confusion. She fumbles with her bags clumsily before snatching them from the floor. Without excusing herself, she makes her way to the door as they both watch in even more confusion.

The moment that she's out of the bar, Bugsy stands up hastily. He backpedals away from them as he peeks around the bar nervously. He feels like the walls of the bar are closing in on him making him feel claustrophobic. "Pepe, I will call you tomorrow," he says as he makes his way to the bar. Not only does it feel like the walls of the bar were closing in on him, it feels as if the walls of the

71

world are closing in on him. The reality that they will not be able to get away from their problems has finally set in. He now understands that they may be able to run, but they will never be able to hide.

ELEVEN

The Next Morning...

Bugsy and Shontay drive in total silence. The radio has been off the entire ride and neither of them has said a word. They're both caught up in their own thoughts. Seeing Shontay on television last night was unreal and a rude awakening for them. He wishes he could tell her that things will be okay, but even he doesn't believe that. One thing they both know is that once they are caught, they can kiss their freedom goodbye forever. That alone is the motivation for the both of them to never get caught. Being able to run forever sounds good, but they both realize that the chances of that are very slim.

"Babe," he says breaking the silence. She looks over to him with desperation in her eyes, hoping that he has a method to the madness. "I apologize for all of this. If you want to give up I understand. I'm the criminal not you. I would be selfish to expect you to keep this chase going. The reality is we can't do this forever. Me, I have no plans of them taking me alive. I already made my mind up. Whatever I have to do to stay free I will. Even if that means dying trying to stay free. I know that's not your life," he says with stern eyes. "So, if you ready to throw in the towel, I can't be mad at you."

"Throw in the towel?" she asks. "Yeah, go ahead and turn yourself in."

"Turn myself in and then what? Spend the rest of my life in prison?" she cries. He sits in silence, not having an answer for her. As much as he would love to tell her that won't be the case, he refuses to lie to her. He's never lied to her in the past. Regardless of the situation, no matter how much the truth may have hurt her, he's always kept it real with her. From confessing to murders to confessing about girls he's cheated with, he's always given her the absolute truth. He knows that she's looking for a dispute from him, claiming that won't be the case, but instead of lying to her he chooses to stay quiet.

30 Minutes Later...

He cruises through the country roads of Dover Downs. They both look around, astonished at their surroundings. They feel as if they're in the deep country so much further away from the city life they just left minutes ago. He slows the car down as he approaches the address on the paper that he's reading from. He spots Domingo sitting on the raggedy house a few feet away.

"Come on," he instructs as he grabs the shopping bag from underneath his seat.

Shontay sits on the edge of the seat as she flips the visor down. She stares into the mirror into her eyes and sees a total stranger. Her once beautiful eyes are now deeply sunk in with misery lying in them. Dark circles and big bags seep under them from days of crying and no sleep. She adjusts the blonde wig on her head before putting on huge dark sunglasses not only to cover her misery, but to disguise herself as well.

Bugsy led the way to the porch as she follows close behind. Domingo welcomes them into the apartment with open arms. The inside of the apartment is more beat up than the exterior of the house. Filth covers the apartment from wall to wall.

They shake hands firmly. "Glad you came through as you said you would," Domingo says with a bright smile.

"I'm a man of my word. I said I would so I do. Brought a kilo through," he says as he taps the shopping bag. "To get this thing started now I hope you are a man of your word."

"All I have is my word. I'm flat broke," he says with a bigger smile.

"Dig this, me and you don't know each other from a can of paint. I'm trusting that you can do all that you said you can do. I'm also trusting that I will have no trouble getting mines back. I don't take losses well. If I lose, everybody loses, dig me?"

"I'm not about losses. I'm about gains, big gains."

"Enough said," Bugsy says as he raises his fist in the air for a fist bump. "Well, let's gain then."

TWELVE

Two Weeks Later...

Bugsy sits in his regular seat next to Jack who is high out of his mind right now. His eyes are glassy and his mouth is twisted like a stroke victim from the excessive amount of cocaine that he's snorted. Even with the twitching, his mouth has been running twenty miles a minute.

"I'm ready for you," he says. "Tomorrow we get together in my office and do it all over again."

Bugsy looks over at Jack with a face full of agitation. "Jack, Jack, I got you. You said the same shit over and over a hundred times already. Fall back, relax," he says as he looks away from Jack.

"Sorry, sorry. I just want to make sure everything will go as I plans. It will be the same stuff though, right?"

A strange feeling comes over Bugsy causing him to totally ignore Jack as hard as that is. He feels a strong vibe coming from across the bar. He stares over the bar onto what his senses has attracted him to. A slender white middle-age man sits at the bar attempting to be discreet. Bugsy knows this feeling quite well. Whenever he has felt it in the past, he's never been wrong. He can spot a cop from many miles away.

Bugsy watches as the man stares at the back of the bar over his glass that he holds to his mouth. He looks to the back of the room where Pepe is standing close to one of the dancers. She steps closer to him staring into his eyes seductively. With one hand, she grabs hold of his collar while clasping Pepe's hand with the other. As discreet as they think they are, the transaction is quite evident. The woman walks away as Pepe tucks the money she gave him into his pocket.

Damn, Bugsy thinks to himself as his eyes bounces back onto the man across the bar. He needs to get over to Pepe to warn him but he can't take the chance of getting caught up in it. The man picks up his phone from the bar and starts to dial. Bugsy automatically thinks he's calling for back up. He can clearly envision the police bombarding their way into the bar any minute now. The last thing he wants is to be in here when they come. Although he is only a patron, he doesn't know if he can trust Pepe enough to hold it down.

"Jack," Bugsy says as he gets up from his seat. He slides the seat under the bar as he keeps his eyes locked onto the man. "Listen, go back there and tell Pepe shit looking crazy in here. Tell him to shut down business for the night and break out of here. I got a feeling the police gonna bust in here any minute now. There's an undercover in the building."

Jack peeks around quite paranoid, blowing their cover. "Undercover where?" he asks in a panic.

He quickly captures the attention of the man who sits across the bar. He stares at them through his sneaky and beady eyes. Bugsy tries to play it cool by smiling a nervous grin.

Bugsy gets more than nervous as Pepe makes his way across the bar toward them. He counts through a hefty stack of money in the wide open for everyone to see. With the flicking of each bill, Bugsy gets even more nervous and backpedals away from the bar as Jack grabs hold of his arm.

"Don't worry about no police. I have them in my pocket. They will never come into this bar," he says in a cocky manner.

Bugsy snatches away from him with great force and continues on his way. As soon as Pepe gets within an arm's reach of Bugsy, he extends the stack of bills to him. Bugsy peeks through the corner of his eye at the man who has his eyes glued onto them.

"Here is two grand," Pepe whispers only loud enough for them to hear.

Bugsy shakes his head from side to side, giving Pepe the eye. He touches both of them on the shoulder one by one. "Yo, I'm out."

He turns around with no further conversation and speed-walks toward the door. Jack stands at the bar in confusion as Pepe tails behind Bugsy. With each step, Bugsy picks up the pace, watching over his shoulder at the man who is now getting up out of his seat as well.

He pushes the door open and as soon as the door closes behind him, he takes off in flight. Pepe steps out of the bar seconds later and without knowing the reason, he takes off running behind Bugsy from a nearby alley. They both watch the door where the man now stands. He looks up and down the block quite puzzled. Seconds later, what is seen is confirmation to what Bugsy already suspected. The man steps toward an unmarked car in which another man sits in the driver's seat.

"Just as I figured," he says as he points to the car. "A fucking pig," he spits with vengeance. "You was this fucking close to getting us all locked the fuck up in there tonight. He was watching every fucking move you made. You got away tonight, but now they're going to be on your ass."

THIRTEEN

The Next Morning...

Bugsy and Shontay step into Jack's office to close the second kilo deal with Jack. Bugsy was expecting Jack to be wired and anxious, but instead he sits at his desk with a long distraught face. An uncomfortable feeling overcomes Shontay as she feels Jack damn near look through her. Through her dark sunglasses, she peeks at him as he tilts his head, looking at her from every angle.

"Jack, my boy! What's going on with you? You look like your wife just left you or something. Everything alright?"

Jack stares in front of him in space looking as if he's seen a ghost. He shakes his head for seconds before uttering a word. "No, Mike. I wish it was but it's not," he says before shaking his head in silence again.

"Talk to me. What's the problem? Who fucking with you?" Bugsy asks with a playful grin.

"It's not about me," Jack replies. "It's y'all," he says pointing to the both of them.

"Us?" Bugsy asks in surprise. "What about us?"

"It's about last night?"

"What about last night?" Bugsy asks in a high pitch voice crackling with nervousness. "Did they get Pepe?"

"No, Pepe is okay. I just talked to him five minutes ago." He becomes silent once again. "Those cops were not there for Pepe or no drug sting. They were there looking for her," he says pointing his finger at Shontay.

Shontay's knees buckle at the sound of his words. Bugsy looks at her catching her in his grip and holding her tight. He smiles at Jack attempting to play a mind game on him. "Looking for her for what?" he asks. "Jack, you must be bugging."

"I'm not bugging. I know all about everything. In fact, everybody knows all about everything," he says with fear written all over his face. "They've been in the bar flashing her picture around and asking questions.

Bugsy continues on with the game. "Her picture? Questions about what?"

"Questions about her whereabouts. Said that she's wanted for the murder of three cops in New Jersey."

"Lies, Jack. That's all lies. They got my baby mixed up Jack," he says as he squeezes Shontay's shoulder with a false sense of comfort. He can clearly see that Jack isn't buying his story. Shontay flops with fear as she attempts to stand there as nonchalant as she possibly can.

Bugsy stares at her with compassion before turning back to look at Jack. As he stares at Jack, a feeling of suspicion comes over him. He whispers to Shontay as he gently pushes her toward the couch. "Take a seat."

He peeks around at the spacious office with a suspect look on his face. He backs up a few steps and locks the door. As he's making his way over to the bathroom door, he draws one of his guns from his waistband. He snatches the door open with his gun aimed into bathroom.

Jack watches in complete shock. A fearful look covered his face as Bugsy walked toward him. He keeps his eyes glued onto the shiny chrome handgun, not even blinking. "Mike, Mike," he stutters.

"Jack, my boy," he says with a devious grin. "Why do I get the feeling that this is a set up?" he says as he plants the gun onto Jack's shoulder.

He stares into his eyes as he makes his way over to the huge picture window. Jack swivels his chair around to keep his eyes on Bugsy.

Bugsy's gun is still aimed at his head. "If this is a set up, you will never make it out of here alive. They bust into these doors and I'm splattering your brains all over this office."

He looks around outside in search of any suspicious vehicles as he draws the shades closed tight. Shontay watches from the couch in suspense wondering what move Bugsy will make next.

"A set up?" Jack asks with confusion on his face. "If who come busting in?"

Bugsy walks over with fury on his face. "The heat," he replies.

He snatches Jack by the collar and shoves the barrel of his gun into Jack's mouth. "Did they get you to bring us in?"

"Mike, I would never do that. I don't fuck with the police. You should know better than that. My entire business thrives off of dirty money. I'm a crook just like y'all. I mean just like you," he rephrases while peeking over at Shontay.

"My baby ain't no fucking crook. I told you its all lies."

"Look, whatever is going on I don't know and I don't even care. It ain't my business. Our business is powder and that's all I care about. I'm with you. Whatever I have to do to prove that to you I will."

Bugsy snatches Jack's shirt open, looking for a wire.

Jack is taken aback. "Mike, what's wrong?"

Bugsy stands in silence for seconds. "You got the money?"

"Yes, right here in my desk. Can I reach and get it?"

"Go ahead," Bugsy says as he watches Jack closely.

Jack reaches into his desk slowly and retrieves the leather sachet case. "Here, fifty-five large."

Bugsy snatches the case from him and quickly unzips it. He skims over the bills quickly before looking over to Shontay. "Gimme the bag," he commands.

Shontay races over and hands him the bag. Bugsy slams the bag onto the desk. "Now walk us out of the building," he says as he snatches him out of his seat. "We walk out here and any sight of cops, I'm blasting you with no hesitation. There will be a blood bath before they take us."

Minutes Later...

Shontay leads the way to their getaway car as Bugsy walks with his arm around Jack's shoulders. He holds his gun close to Jack's side as he peeks around cautiously. Not a cop is in clear view. Bugsy instructs Shontay to get in the car first and once she's in safely, he pushes Jack away and gets in to the driver's seat. He rolls the window down and speaks to Jack who stands petrified at the curb.

"Jack, it's us against them," he utters. "Remember, your life depends on our safety. From this point on, you are my eyes and my ears. Anything look funny or sound funny to you, you better let me know. Got me?"

"Mike, I promise you, anything that I hear you will be the first person that I contact. Just do me a favor and stay away from the bar for a few until things cool off. I don't need them prying into my business. I need you to know that I'm on your side though. You have to trust me."

"You better keep it like that. You're either on my side or on your back."

FOURTEEN

Bugsy scurries as he packs the abundance of clothes that he has accumulated. He pulls the already worn clothes from the drawers and packs them in to shopping bags. He then gathers clothes still with the price tags, and piles all of them together on the floor. He runs over to the wall safe and sets the combination. From the safe, he grabs hold to close to a quarter of a million dollars in cash and the remaining five kilos that he has left.

He has no trust or faith in Jack and believes that he will give him up in a heartbeat. He plans to flee from this hotel without telling Jack. He plans to keep Jack close enough to know exactly what's going on, but far enough wherein he can't give the police any information on him. The fact that he doesn't trust Jack makes him want to get rid of him, but he battles with that because he realizes without Jack, he has no ears in the city of Delaware.

As he's packing the kilos into his duffle bag, a loud crashing in the bathroom causes him great alarm. He freezes in motion as he listens for another sound but there's none. He drops the bag and runs to the bathroom door, which he forces open. He's shocked to see Shontay sprawled out on the floor, eyes closed, looking as if she isn't even breathing. His heart skips a beat as he stands still, just staring at her for seconds before making a move toward her.

He hovers over her protectively. "Sha!" he shouts as he shakes her with all of his might. Her body flip-flops lifelessly. He places his hands between her breasts and holds them there, hoping to feel her heart beat. He feels her breathing faintly. He shakes her harder.

"Sha, wake up! What the fuck?" he asks fearfully.

Her eyes open slowly and she stares up at him with a blank look on her face. She has no clue of where she is or what has happened.

"What happened?"

She looks around in shock for seconds before she slowly comes to. He lifts her limp body upward and places her against his chest. "Talk to me baby. What's going on?"

She pulls away from him and sits upright. He grabs her hand and lifts her up onto her feet. She stands clumsily and stares into his eyes in a daze.

"What the fuck happened?" he asks.

"I don't know," she replies with uncertainty in her eyes. "All I remember is standing in the mirror fixing my hair and then it all went blank."

"Must be the pressure. It's gotten the best of you. Babe, you gotta chill. This thing will work itself out," he says as a way to bring her sanity. For the very first time in their relationship, he's told her a lie. He hopes the lie makes her feel better. In order to do that, he feels he must add more onto the lie.

"Babe, they know you're innocent in all of this. It's me that they really want. Once they get me you're good. If I turn myself in this nightmare will be over for you. If that's what you want, I will do it," he says knowing good and well he has no plans whatsoever of ever turning himself in. He's just speaking for the moment. He gazes deep into her eyes awaiting her response but she doesn't give him one. "Is that what you want? You want me to turn myself in?"

Silence fills the air for what seems like an eternity. His heart is pounding with anticipation and suspense. She opens her mouth slowly but no words come out.

"Is it?" he asks again. She says not a word in reply. "Babe, answer me."

Still, she doesn't reply verbally but the look in her eyes indicate to him that she may be considering it. "Say no more," he says shaking his head from side to side sympathetically. "The eyes don't lie. I get it. So, I'm in this by myself huh?" he asks, hoping to instill guilt.

"Everything you ever been through in life who been there for you? Me! Mother threw you out in the cold and who let you live with them in my mother's house? Me! When you had no job, who made sure you ate? Me! Who bought all the clothes you had on your back? Me! When all your friends turned their back on you who was a friend to you? Me, that's who!

He sees the guilt spreading across her face so he pours it on thicker. "Even when I didn't have shit, I always made sure you had everything you needed. Whatever I had to do to provide for you, I did! And now you turn your back on me? Whenever you had a battle, it was me and you against the world. Now I have a battle and it's just me against the world. I get it," he says while biting down onto his bottom lip.

Shontay drowns in guilt. As crazy as it is for him to compare his battles with hers, she still feels bad. She sits back speechless.

"When shit goes bad for you, you really find out who got your back. It's cool though because I got my own back!"

FIFTEEN

Two Hours Later...

Shontay rides shotgun in a trancelike state the same way she's been for what now seems like an eternity. She's still feeling woozy and weak from her episode. Confused about it all, she charges it off as too much stress. She's never been under this much pressure in her life and it's taking a toll on her.

She's heard Bugsy speak the entire ride but has no comprehension of what he he's been saying. Really, she hasn't been paying any attention to him because there's nothing he can say to make sense of any of this. Thoughts of turning herself in occupy her mind. Although she's told him that she wouldn't give in because of him, deep down inside she knows that's only partly true. The main reason she won't turn herself in is because she believes if she did, she would be left to fight this battle all alone. Although she's sure the end results will be the same, she finds strength in having him by her side.

An hour ago they checked into a rinky-dink motel for the time being. Bugsy is running out of escape plans and is now just playing it all by the moment. It seems to him that every move that he thought was a good move, proves to end up a bigger obstacle standing in front of him. Even with all the odds stacked against them, giving up and turning himself in is not an option.

They pull up to Domingo's house and a widespread of in and out traffic catches their attention. They both recognize it as drug traffic. The clientele here is totally different from the clientele back at the bar. At the bar, there were functional addicts with careers. These people here all appear to be junkies and crack addicts. Poor white trailer trash is the proper term for them. Tracked arm, blonde haired, prostitutes make up most of the traffic. Just at the sight of it all, Bugsy realizes that it will be hard for them to blend in and camouflage themselves.

He bangs on the door and a young Mexican girl opens it slowly. They walk right past her. What was on the outside of the house is only a fraction of what is going on inside. Domingo stands in the center of the living-room, running a full blown drug operation. He peeks up at them as he continues to make sale after sale to the dozen and a half customers that are lurking in the room. Just as he clears one batch of customers out of the room, another batch refills the room with no break in the action.

"It's been like this all day," Domingo says with a bright smile. "I'm gonna make us rich."

Shontay makes her way over to the couch in the corner just to get away from the action. As she steps, her knees buckle. She catches herself mid-step before losing her ground and tumbling over on to the couch face-first. Her sudden fall catches everyone off-guard.

The room become still as they all watch her. Bugsy watches in shock before taking off in her direction. He flips her body over and she flops like a rag doll. His heart beat with terror as he calls her name.

"Sha," he says as he slaps her gently across the face. He gets no response from her so he smacks her harder and harder. "Sha, please!" he shouts with desperation. "Wake up Sha."

She's breathing faintly but still is not responding. He felt helpless. She seems to be less conscience than the she was during the previous episode. For a second, he even believes that she's stopped breathing.

"Somebody call 911!" he shouts without thought. As he considers the matter at hand, he recalls that decision. He know 9.1.1., are the last numbers that they need at this time. "No, don't call! Somebody help me get her to the car.

"Everybody out!" Domingo shouts as he runs over to aid Bugsy. Together, they lifts her limp body from the couch. She weighs just barely 125 pounds, but her dead weight makes her feel like she weighs a ton. They dump her body into the backseat, and slam the doors shut. "Domingo, point me to the nearest hospital."

SIXTEEN

Two Hours Later...

Bugsy paces the floor in the hall of the hospital. His nerves are a wreck between worrying about Shontay and watching the door for any sign of the police. Shontay used an alias, but still he worries that maybe they will know who she is. The sooner they're out of this hospital, the better.

A familiar nurse walks toward him. He tries to read the expression on her face but it's blank. He rushes toward her and meets her in the middle of the hall.

"You can come in the room now," she says with no indicating facial expression.

"Is she okay? What's wrong with her?"

"The doctor is waiting for you," she says making him even more nervous.

He takes off, leaving the nurse standing there. He stands at the door quite hesitant to step inside. He pushes the door gently and peeks his head inside before stepping in. He finds Shontay laying

100

on the bed, fully conscious, just staring into space. The doctor looks up from his paperwork at Bugsy's entrance.

"Sha, what up?"

She never looks at him not once, as if he isn't there. "Doc, what's the deal? Is she alright?"

"She's fine," he replies with a smile.

"She's gotta take better care of herself. She's a human ball of stress. Blood pressure is at level three."

Bugsy sighs relief just hearing, what he views as simple. He truly feels as if high blood pressure is nothing. High blood pressure is as common in the ghetto as welfare. Damn near everybody he knows has high blood pressure.

"That's it, high blood pressure?"

The doctor displays a stern look. "That's it? That's more than enough. Six hundred thousand people die every year from high blood pressure. That's no good for her or the baby," the doctor says as he looks away with disgust.

Bugsy replays the words in his head over and over, thinking he's heard wrong. "Huh? Baby, what are you talking about?"

"Yes, baby. You heard right. Congratulations, you're going to be a father," he says with a bright smile. "Now take care of mommy and try not to stress her out anymore."

"Baby," Bugsy repeats again, trying to make it settle in.

The doctor chuckles. "Yes, get it through your head, dad. She's a high risk pregnancy due to her pressure. We will monitor her throughout the pregnancy but she doesn't need any more stress."

Just when he thought things couldn't get any worse they just did. He shakes his head in despair. He looks over to Shontay and for the first time, their eyes meet. She shakes her head in defeat. Confusion covers her face.

"We are gonna keep her here overnight just to watch her and make sure everything is okay which I'm sure it will be," he says as he makes his way toward the door. "Be back in a few hours," he says before closing the door behind him.

Bugsy walks over to Shontay and without saying a word, he hugs her tightly. She buries her head in his chest as she sobs away.

"Why?" she cries. "Why is all this happening to me? What did I do to deserve all of this?"

Bugsy feels horrible that he has not an answer for her. He just tightens the hug for reassurance that he can't even promise her.

"I can't answer that, but what I do know is that we gotta get outta here. Get your stuff together, we gotta go."

"Go? Go where?"

"Outta here! You can't stay here overnight and take the risk of the heat coming here and nabbing you. We gotta roll."

"Babe, I'm pregnant! I'm sick with high blood pressure. I can fall out and die," she whines. "This is over. I can't go anymore. I'm four weeks pregnant. No way can I be on the run not getting prenatal care. I can't even use my real name," she sobs. "I have no choice but to get an abortion," she says as her eyes widen. "I will have to. This is too much," she cries.

Bugsy snaps at the words that just escaped her mouth. "Abortion? I don't kill my babies. You fucking crazy?"

"No, you're fucking crazy! You think we can have a baby on the run. How will that go? We have no insurance. We can't use our real names."

"Shhh," he says as he covers her mouth and looks around to make sure no one has come into the room and heard her. "We got money! Fuck insurance!"

"You just don't get it. This ain't one of your gangster movies you watch over and over. This is real life. When those movies are over and the credits roll, they go on and live their real lives. When this movie is over and the credits roll, we are going to jail for the rest of our lives," she says before sobbing away.

He rolls the IV stand closer to her. "Here take this out. We gotta go. Come on," he demands.

"Baby, I'm scared. This has to stop."

"Me too," he admits for the very first time in his life. "But it can't stop. We gotta keep going. We got too much riding on it. Now let's go."

SEVENTEEN

3:15 Am / Days Later...

The bar has just closed and Jack sits in the driver's seat of his Porsche Panamera. Speaking from the passenger's seat is the bar manager, Charlie.

"If not exactly in the bar all day, they're somewhere close just waiting on my call. They know they're here in this city and they're not leaving until they get her."

Jack trembles like a leaf but he tries to play it calm. "But why, Charlie? Fucking why?" he whines. "Why did you even get involved? Why did you make the call? When did you make the call?"

Charlie smiles as if he has done a good thing. "I'm so smooth that I made the call right as the news was on the screen," he boasts. "I bent down as if I was reaching for a glass and I made the call," he smiles. "Nobody ever saw a thing."

"Again, but why?"

"Why Jack? A woman who just killed three cops was in the bar just a few feet away from me, from us. I didn't know what her next move was gonna be. We all could've been next. It was a humanitarian act, Jack."

"So, now you expecting some type of humanitarian award or something? If you were smart as you think you are you would have at least waited until they posted a reward and made it beneficial for yourself."

"You know, I thought about that," he says with a smile. "But it's okay. I done a good thing and someday, I will get my re..," he says before being interrupted by the opening of the back door. He looks into the backseat in surprise and his face becomes pale white as his eyes set on Bugsy.

Bugsy wears a devilish smirk on his face, staring coldly into Charlie's eyes. "Didn't expect to see me ever again, huh?"

Charlie looks over to Jack. "Jack, what's going on?"

Instinctively he reaches for the door handle. Jack locks it quickly.

"Pull off Jack," Bugsy commands.

Jack obeys the command while Charlie fidgets uncontrollably in his seat. Bugsy places the noses of both guns to the back of Charlie's head. "Move again and I will splatter your snitch ass brains all over that windshield."

"Mike, please not in my car, please," he begs.

"Jack," Bugsy says as he aims one of the guns at Jack's head. "Shut the fuck up and drive. That's what the fuck you do. Don't tell me shit! I'm the captain of this fucking ship!" Jack looks straight ahead fearfully and drives as he's been told to.

For the next ten minutes, the only talking in the car is coming from Charlie who is begging desperately for his life. Bugsy manages to block out his begging and crying with the many thoughts that occupy his mind. With all the madness around him, he felt as if Delaware was his serenity. He foolishly thought he could hide here, if not forever, at least long enough to finish his supply of cocaine. He figured with money, he could move to the next phase and come up with a master-plan That was until Charlie here, messed everything up for him.

Bugsy snaps out of his trance as they cruises down what he believes to be the perfect block. "Slow down Jack. Right here, right here," he shouts hastily.

"No! Please don't do this! Jack, don't let him do this to me!"

"Charlie, I can't help you. You done this to yourself," Jack replies with compassion in his eyes.

"Stop Jack!" Bugsy shouts.

Jack slams on the brakes and looks in to the backseat. "Please, Mike, not in my car!" he begs once again disregarding Bugsy's threat.

Bugsy forces the door open and climbs out. He snatches the passenger door open and drags the squirming and fighting Charlie out of the car. He drags him just like a rag-doll into the dark alley. In seconds, the block is illuminated by the sparks of guns. The alley lights up consecutively for seconds. Jack counts the shots by the sparks of illumination. Altogether, he's counted over 20 shots. Jack's heart is saddened even more as he envisions his longtime acquaintance lying dead in a pool of blood.

Bugsy steps casually out of the alley as if he hasn't just executed Charlie. As he steps toward the car, Jack has a good mind to leave Bugsy there, but his fear won't let him step on the gas pedal. He gets into the car, slams the door shut, and without looking over, he speaks in a calm tone.

"Go."

Jack fumbles clumsily with the pedals as he pulls off. The car stops abruptly, frustrating Bugsy to no end.

"What the fuck you doing?"

"Sorry, sorry," he apologizes to save his life. "I made a mistake." Bugsy looks away with agitation covering his face. "Mike, what's going on? You're making matters worse for yourself. You just slaughtered a man in cold blood. This may be all normal for you, but I'm no killer. You just made me an accessory to a murder."

"Jack, we are in this thing together. It ain't about me no more. It's about US, me and you," he says with a satanic smirk. "Remember that."

EIGHTEEN

Days Later...

Bugsy stares at Shontay as he slams the gear into park.

"Dig, when we get in here don't utter a word to these motherfuckers. We gonna get this money and be out. I'm gon' need your eyes in here so watch carefully," he says as he grabs the duffel-bag from under the seat. "Let's go."

Bugsy leads the way toward Domingo's house as Shontay trots behind him. Both of them scan the area cautiously. As they step onto the porch, the door is opened for them. Domingo opens the door wider, inviting them in. Bugsy steps inside confidently. His eyes automatically land on the two unknown men who sit on the couch. Their eyes land onto the duffel-bag.

"Mike, this is Money," Domingo says as he points to the man who sits on the couch glistening with diamond jewelry.

"Money, this my man Mike. And that's Hammer, over there," he says pointing to the man sitting next to him. Bugsy doesn't even acknowledge him. He and Money stare at each other, trying to get a feel of one another.

Money smile a comforting smile. Bugsy replies with a cold head nod as he breezes past them. Quickly, they both look Shontay up and down making her feel uncomfortable. As she passes them, they stare at her behind with perversion. Hammer grabs a handful of his manhood as he nudges Money.

Domingo walks over to Bugsy and begins whispering. "They only want one now."

"One? I thought they wanted two. Got me riding around with this shit for nothing," he says with attitude. He looks over to the men on the couch who are both watching him closely. "That's bad business. Where I'm from, you do what you say you gon' do. Y'all said two."

"Where y'all from?" Money asks trying to break the ice and ease the tension.

"That's neither here nor there," he replies. It ain't where you from, it's where you at, right?"

"Agreed," Money replies.

"Let's get to the meeting at hand."

"No doubt," Money replies as he grabs hold of the shopping bag that's laying at his feet. "I was telling my man Domingo, the work y'all got is on fire. We can really do some things with that. We can take over the whole Wilmington with it. Nobody won't be able to eat. If you can just give me a little lead-way I can really do some things, feel me?"

Bugsy looks up with a stern look. "Nah, I don't feel you. What you mean?"

"I mean, if you match me brick for brick. If I buy three or four, you front me three or four."

"This the first time we meet and you come at me with consignment? I take that as a total disrespect."

"I mean no disrespect. Just a businessman trying to make a dollar. No more no less."

"Well, let's do business then," Bugsy says as he pulls the brick from the bag. he hands it over to Money who peels the wrapping and examines it closely.

"Yeah, this that shit, right here," he says with joy spread across his face. He hands the brick over to Hammer to take a peek. He quickly hands the bag of money over. Bugsy peels a stack from the bag, lays the bag down and immediately starts counting."

"It's all there bro, not a dollar missing. My money good. Counted it four times, myself."

Like an experienced bank teller Bugsy rips through the money in a matter of minutes. He stacks it all back into the bag. He looks over to Domingo and gives him a head nod before making his way out of the room. Domingo follows behind.

While Money is staring at the work mesmerized, his partner, Hammer is mesmerized by Shontay.

"Shorty," he whispers.

Shontay ignores him without even looking at his way.

"Shorty," he calls again.

Shontay looks over to him with disgust on her face.

"That's your dude?" he asks.

Shontay looks away as if he's not even worthy of an answer.

"What, you can't talk?" he asks with sarcasm. "He must got you trained." Both he and Money laugh hysterically.

With persistence, he continues on. "That's your dude?" he asks just as Bugsy is walking into the room. Shontay looks up upon his entrance. The man stares at Bugsy with the words still in his mouth.

"What's that?" Bugsy asks with a jealous smirk.

"Nothing, I was talking to her," he replies staring into his eyes with no fear.

"Don't ask her shit. You wanna know something, ask me. Anything you can ask her in my absence, you should be able to ask her in my presence. Don't wait until I leave the room."

"I was asking if she was your lady or not. I didn't want to be rude and say something outta pocket."

"She walked in with me so you already outta pocket."

"Nah, not really. It's a free world. You see a pretty woman and if you like what you see you go for it. That's what men do right?"

He's pressing Bugsy's buttons, but Bugsy manages to keep his cool.

"You're right, it's a free world. Men do what they gone do, but when they do what they do, they gotta be prepared for the repercussions. For every action there's a reaction."

"Anything I do, I'm prepared for the repercussions," he replies with sarcasm.

Money sits back in silence just watching how it all plays out. Deep down inside, he wants to know what and who they're working with which is why he has yet to intervene.

That remark is like the straw that broke the camel's back. Bugsy takes two sidesteps before leaping across the room at the Hammer, gun already drawn. Hammer backs up with fear, not expecting the attack. Bugsy rests the gun on his head. You ready for this reaction?"

"Hold, hold," Money says as he stands up trying to pry in between the two of them.

Shontay stands up nervously. "Babe, no."

Bugsy forces his forearm against Money's throat. "You don't know me so don't touch me!" He looks at the man as he keeps his side-eye on Hammer. "I will murder you if you ever disrespect me again." He slams the man down onto the couch. "That's my first and last warning."

Money and his partner sit back in silence, barely breathing out of fear of his next move. "A few things in life I will murder over and that's my money and my wife. Keep the money right and keep your eyes off my wife and we won't have no problems."

"Bro, it's all a misunderstanding. He was outta pocket, you're right. We don't want no problems. All we wanna do is get money."

"Well, let's not misunderstand each other again and let's get money."

Money nods his head. "Understood."

With no further words, Bugsy tucks his gun back into his waistband and makes his way across the room. He plants a reassuring hand on Shontay's shoulder and they exit the apartment, leaving everyone in silence.

NINETEEN

Three Days Later...

Bugsy lays back on the bed fully dressed while waiting for Shontay to get dressed and ready. He's quite anxious to get outside on the count that he has Money from Wilmington waiting on him to buy another kilo. He flips through the channels just to kill time. Shontay steps out of the bathroom with not a stitch of clothing on. The only material in sight is the towel that she has covering her hair.

For a second, he gets caught up in the beauty of her tender body. Beads of water trickle down her smooth caramel skin arousing him immensely. As his eyes land on her belly, he gets caught up in the fact that a baby version of him is inside of there. That gives him a feeling that he's never felt before. He still can't fathom the fact that she will soon be the mother of his child. Under normal circumstances, he would be the happiest man alive. With all that's going on, he can't fully accept and appreciate, nor enjoy it. As he takes one long look at her, he wants to jump on her and make passionate love to her right now, but the money is calling him. For a second he tells himself that the money can wait. Reluctantly, he quickly looks away to take his mind off of her.

He flicks the channels with even more speed until his curiosity is triggered. He flicks back quickly and the words New Jersey flashing across the bottom of the screen causes him great concern. Not a second later, Shontay's Police Academy photo flashes across the screen and fear rips through his body.

He turns the volume up just so he won't miss a single word. He listens on as the reporter states all of the obvious. His ears stretch open wide when the more than obvious is stated. Hearing his government name on national television sounds unreal. His photo is now posted on the screen next to hers. He looks over to Shontay who stands in the middle of the room with her full attention on the television screen as well.

"Authorities believe that Marcus Hansome has taken Rookie Officer Shontay Baker away from the scene and may be holding her captive. The last sighting of the two was in Wilmington Delaware. Sources say before Delaware, the two made a brief stop in Philadelphia."

Footage of Bugsy's cousin being escorted from his home by Federal Agents flashes across the screen. Both Bugsy and Shontay's mouth drops to the floor in surprise. *"A vehicle that was stolen from a rest stop was found at the home of this man."* Bugsy's cousin's photo pops up on the screen. *"From his home, undisclosed amounts of money and cocaine were retrieved,"* the reporter states. The Subaru is shown parked in front of thehouse. *"In a routine traffic stop in this vehicle, an important piece to the puzzle was discovered."*

"Dumb motherfucker!" Bugsy shouts at the screen as he stands to his feet with fury. He looks over to Shontay. "I told him to burn the fucking car and his dumb ass joyriding in it! This motherfucker gave me up. I always knew he had bitch in him."

It all gets worse when Shontay's mother and sister appears on the screen, both in tears. They stand behind a podium as her mother speaks.

"Shontay, baby, if you're alive and watching this, please somehow give us a sign. Call us, please. We are worried about you. Baby, we won't stop searching for you until you're home with us," she says before breaking down into tears. "We are praying for you every second of the day."

Shontay watches with tears of her own as her sister consoles her mother.

Bugsy turns off the television with rage. He lowers his head with a loss of words. After seconds of silence he looks up to her. He grabs her by her waist and pulls her close. He stares into her eyes. "There you go Sha. You got your out."

"What?" she asks.

"You out," he whispers with defeat in his voice. "They think I'm holding you hostage. You're innocent babe and they know it. Give yourself up and you can walk away from all of this and live happily ever after."

"You really believe that?" she asks.

Bugsy nods his head up and down. "Of course you will have to give me up and even make it sound believable, but I think it can be done. After all, I did drag you with me. It's the truth."

Shontay stares into his eyes with deep thought at what he's saying to her. She wonders if it all could end that simple. But then, her sense of loyalty to him kicks in. The fact that she will have to tell them he kidnapped her doesn't sit well with her. She knows that a kidnap charge could get him another twenty years added to any amount of time that they already have in store for him.

"All you have to do is say the word and I will drop you off at the nearest police precinct. Just give me time to take all my stuff outta here and strategize my next move. Somehow, I will have the money sent to you for lawyer fees to fight your way outta this shit."

"But what about you?" she asks with sadness in her eyes. "What are you gonna do?"

"Me? I gotta keep it pushing. Ain't no pot of gold at the end of this rainbow for me. I ain't got a clean shot at freedom. I'm riding this runaway train until it rolls off the track. Your destiny is in your own hands at this point. It's all on you from here. What is it gonna be? You with me or you out?"

TWENTY

Two Days Later...

Bugsy stares into the mirror at his reflection. He sees traces of stress all over his face. He's been under pressure all of his life. From being dead broke and homeless to fighting murder charges. He feels that he's experienced all that life has to offer. Even with all of that, he's never cracked. He's been able to hold it down wearing his poker face, not letting the world know how much pressure he was really under.

This pressure is quite different though because normally he's fighting his battles alone. Having Shontay with him adds a burden onto his shoulders that he's never carried. With him alone, he'd be able to keep it moving, only worrying about himself. All her crying and complaining is really taking toll on him.

He normally never has regrets with any decision that he's ever made but this is one that he wishes he wouldn't have made. He constantly reminds

126

himself that he can't harbor on what he should have done. He has to deal with the situation at hand. He replays a conversation that he had with a dope-fiend one time who told him that for every bad decision you make, it takes three or four good decisions to correct the bad one. It seems to him that every decision that he's made so far, that he thought was a good one, turned out to be an even worse one.

For the very first time in his life, he's considered giving up. Quitting is something that he doesn't believe in, but this is the closest that he's ever been to actually doing it. He has to remind himself every moment of the days that he cannot quit just to inspire himself to keep it moving. Picturing himself in shackles in some prison's cage was all the motivation he needs to keep going.

With them close on his heels, he knows that he has to stay ten steps ahead of them. Although he understood the seriousness of the matter all the while, seeing his picture on television put things in a total different perspective for him. A deeper reality set in once he realized they know who he is. It was then that he was able to fully place himself in Shontay's shoes and understand exactly what she was going through. Before then, he was able to selfishly charge it off as her almost overreacting.

He realizes that in order to keep the chase going, he will have to make some changes. He plans to relocate from Delaware. Where though, he has not a clue. He also understands that his cousin's car is as hot as a firecracker. He's sure his cousin told them all that he knows, which is why he ditched the car last night.

Stuck here with no wheels makes it impossible to carry on. He feels like a sitting duck, just sitting here in the motel waiting for them to track them down. He doesn't trust Jack the least bit but he has no choice but to call on him for a favor. By force if he has to, he plans on getting Jack to rent him a car to move around in.

He stands at the bathroom sink, ready to make the biggest change. He places the barber's clippers to his head, holds his breath, closes his eyes and in seconds, the clippers snatch his locks out from the root. He runs the clippers over his head, path by path. When he looks up, he sees a reflection of someone that he hasn't seen in close to ten years.

He doesn't see Bugsy 2 Gunz. He sees Marcus. Marcus is the troubled and misguided child who was willing to do anything to fit in and be accepted. Growing up with no father, nor male figure to look up to, he practically raised himself.

He looks deeper into his eyes and sees a pain and hurt that he hasn't seen since he was a child. That hurt is a result of a child whose mother never showed her love to him. He came third to her drug addiction, right behind the love she had for any man that could provide drugs for her. That pain led him to lash out and cause pain to others. Causing others pain always had a way of alleviating his own pain. Hiding behind the mask for so many years, he's forgotten who Marcus really was. He shakes his head and closes his eyes to shake away all the memories of Marcus. He opens his eyes and Marcus is still there. He looks onto the floor at his thick locks and there he finds his strength, his security blanket.

There he stands, feeling naked without his mask. The superhero strength that he's psyched himself up to believe he possesses is now gone. He feels exposed, not even feeling of himself. He doesn't feel like Bugsy 2 Gunz. He feels like plain old Marcus Hansome, a dude he mentally buried many years ago.

With no mask, no cape, no superhero strength, he realizes that he must dig deep into his inner strength and keep the chase going. He stares into the mirror for seconds without blinking.

"Let's get it."

TWENTY-ONE

Three Days Later / 7:00 P.M.

Domingo has just called Bugsy with urgency in his voice. He isn't sure of the details of the urgency, but whatever it is, sounds as if a lot of money could be involved. Whenever Domingo makes emergency calls like this, it's usually about a deal that he can't cover.

"Wait right here babe. Let me go see what he's talking about and I will be right back," he says as he gets out of the fairly new Lincoln MKZ.

The car is compliments of Jack. Bugsy practically had to force Jack to rent him the car yesterday. A reminder that he really has no choice was the determining factor of why he eventually agreed to it. Bugsy hates to keep using force against him because he knows that too much force will eventually break a scared man. Although he bared witness to that he has no other choice but to put the pressure on Jack. He has no one else.

130

Shontay watches him walk away with sadness. Ever since the news report he's been in her ear about turning herself in. Up until hearing them speak of her innocence, he thought she had no way out. Now that he realizes she has an out, he wants her out. He understands how selfish it would be to keep her entangled in this disaster.

She hasn't told him yet, but she's already made her mind up as well. As much as she loves him, she believes that she must get herself out of this. She loves him dearly, but the love blinders has been removed from her eyes. She now has to think about what's best for her and spending the rest of her life in prison is not even a thought at this point. She fears walking into the precinct, but she understands that she will have to take the first step in order to attempt to clear her name; if that is even possible. She realizes that it's a huge risk, but she is almost sure that she's ready to take it.

Before turning herself in, she will be sure to secure the money that he's promised her for an attorney. She just isn't sure how to get the money to her family to hold for her as of yet. Praying that all goes well with that, her very next step will be to abort the baby despite the fact that he made her promise to keep it. He gave her a long song and dance about how he can't leave this world without leaving a child behind to carry out his legacy. Although she agreed and promised him, nothing in this world is going to make her bring a baby into this world with no father.

Bugsy rings the bell, and in a matter of seconds the door opens. Domingo's girlfriend stands at the door with a perplexed look on her face but he pays very little attention to it and steps right in. As soon as he's inside, the door slams shut behind him. He peeks over his shoulder and to his surprise, he stares right into the barrel of a semi-automatic handgun. Holding the gun is Money.

"Don't move nigga," he says through clenched teeth.

A fucking set up," he mumbles to himself. "Fucking Domingo set me up."

He peeks to the far end of the room where he sees Domingo being dragged by Hammer at gunpoint. Domingo's hands are tied together and his mouth is taped shut. Bugsy stares into his eyes and realizes that Domingo is innocent. The fear on his face is a clear indication that he's not behind the caper.

Hammer slams Domingo to the floor and quickly aims his gun at Bugsy.

"Hands in the air motherfucker!"

A smirk covers his face as he thinks back to the day that Bugsy put the gun to his head. A sense of satisfaction fills his heart. For the sake of pure revenge, he wants to pull the trigger and blow his head clean off of his shoulders but he refrains himself thinking of the reward.

Bugsy can't believe that this is happening. He's always been the man behind the gun. Never has he been the victim of a jux. He raises his hands in the air slowly.

****

On the outside, Shontay sits in the car in deep thought when her police instincts led her to a man who is sitting on the next porch. She can't put her finger on it, but something about him makes her feel weird. He peeks around on continuous alert. He looks up and down the block. Finally, his eyes set on her and he doesn't remove them, not even to blink. The look in his eyes brings her discomfort. She looks away from him out of fear, but she continues to peek at him through her peripheral.

****

Bugsy's sees his life flash before his eyes as Hammer walks toward him. He believes from the bottom of his heart that there's no way that they will allow him to walk away from here. In no way does he plan to go down without a fight though. Suddenly, he thinks of Shontay sitting on the outside and what they may do to her after murdering him. Those thoughts make him realize that he has no choice but to bust a move to save the both of their lives.

"Hold up y'all. Easy," he says. "I will give y'all whatever y'all want," he says as he peeks over his shoulder at the gun that's aimed at his head. Not two seconds later, with great accuracy, he flings his elbow high in the air, knocking the gun away from his head. He slides under Money's arm and like a skilled wrestler, he ends up behind him.

Just as Hammer is running over to them, Bugsy manages to turn Money's own gun against his head.

"Stop or he's dead," he threatens as he grips his finger over Money's finger on the trigger. Hammer stops in his tracks.

Inconspicuously, he slides his hand to his side and with the quickness, he draws his gun and aims at the man who stands less than five feet away from him. He now has both of them at gunpoint.

The scales are evened. He and Hammer stare into each other's eyes with their guns aimed at each other's heads.

"Listen this gon' get ugly and nobody will walk away from this. Put your gun down and I will let both of y'all go," he claims. "I been robbing niggasall my life. I believe in karma so I can easily just charge it to the game."

The look in the Hammer's eyes is a look that is Bugsy is totally familiar with. It's the look of no fear. "Listen man, I know what you're thinking but it ain't going down like that. I'm already on the run for the murder of three cops. I don't have shit to lose," he says with a sly smirk. "Let me just go ahead about my business and continue on my mission. Gangster to gangster, we can all just letthis go and forget it ever hap..."

Before he can finish his statement, the sound of gunfire from a .40 caliber rings in the air. The Mexican girl lets out a scream of terror. Bugsy ducks his head low in the nick of time and the bullet spirals into the center of Money's forehead. Bugsy fires a few rounds of his own.

The first shot sends Hammer sailing backwards clumsily. Still holding Money in his grip, he forces him forward using him as his shield. He squeezes continuously at Hammer who has now fallen against the wall. Hammer fires one aimless shot as he collapses onto the floor. He rolls over, body jerking uncontrollably before Bugsy dumps three more into his head.

He throws Money against the wall. With his head gushing with blood, he cries out. "Please don't kill me," he begs. "Please?"

With no verbal response, Bugsy fires two shots, busting his head open like a cantaloupe. As he falls on his face, Bugsy looks around with adrenaline racing through his veins. He runs over to Domingo and stands face to face with him before dumping one in his head. Before his body can even land, Bugsy looks across the room where the Mexican girl is running for cover. As much as he hates to do it, he knows that he can't leave behind any witnesses. He chases behind the girl who is now crawling underneath the couch for safety. He drags her out by her ankle.

BOC!

****

The sound of gunshots send Shontay into a frenzy but fear has her glued to her seat. Her eyes are on the man who is now standing on guard at the porch next door. She knows for sure that

Bugsy's guns have silencers which means the shots fired are not his. She prays that he makes it out of there alive for if he doesn't, she can only imagine her own fate will be the same.

Suddenly Domingo's house door flies open and the sight of Bugsy's face gives her great satisfaction in knowing that he's okay. As he runs down the steps, the man next door stands in confusion. Clearly he didn't expect this outcome. Quickly, he reaches for his weapon.

"Baby, no!" Shontay screams from the car window. As Bugsy watches her with no clue of the man standing a few feet away from him.

BLOCKA! BLOCKA! BLOCKA! BLOCKA!

With great expertise, Shontay squeezes and hit her mark. The man tumbles forward down the steps before he can fire a shot of his own.

Bugsy ducks low as he races to the car, peeking over his shoulder at the wounded man. He hops into the driver's seat and speeds away from the scene of the crime as Shontay stares in shock at her blazing gun. She looks at her registered weapon, realizing that any chance that she had of clearing her name is now over.

She looks up at Bugsy who happens to be staring at her with a pleasing look on his face. "Babe, I always knew you had it in you. Just took the right

situation to bring it outta you. You got my back. I
never once doubted that."

TWENTY-TWO

Two Hours Later / 9:19 P.M.

The Lincoln MKZ is on the shoulder of I-95, disabled with the hood up. It's pitch dark on the highway and traffic is quite heavy. Bugsy is underneath the hood, with not a clue of what he's looking at or looking for. Shontay stands behind, hoping that he can miraculously get the car started. Inside the car is over 250 grand and four kilos which makes it the absolute worst time to be stuck on a highway.

Besides the drugs and money, all of their belongings are packed inside the truck. The shootout in Dover was incentive for them to flee Delaware and never look back. They managed to make an almost bigger mess there than they did back in Newark. They started a fire that they're sure is following them, and they will never be able to put out. They took off with no specific destination. The plan was to just get as far away from Delaware as they possibly can. That was, until the unexpected breakdown.

"Fuck!" Bugsy shouts before kicking the bumper of the car. "A brand new fucking car and it breaks the fuck down!" He paces in small circles as he tries to figure out what to do next.

"Now what?"

"Sha, please!" he shouts furiously as he stares at the oncoming traffic. "We gotta get the fuck off this highway."

He paces around in a panic as he places his hands over his head and stares up at the sky. He refrains himself from throwing a fury tantrum. His fury turns to fear when he spots a State Trooper zooming past them on the opposite side of the highway.

For the first time ever since the start of this ordeal, he looks over to her for an answer. She's dumbfounded.

"We're gonna have to leave the car," he suggests, hoping that she has a better answer for him.

Quickly he thinks of the fact that without a car, they're stuck. "Damn!" he shouts.

He walks to the edge of the shoulder and sticks his thumb in the air like a hitchhiker. He leans over in to the road with desperation, hoping someone will stop.

A second State Trooper passes by on the other side. He watches closely, hoping the Trooper doesn't pay them any attention. Minutes pass and not a single driver even looks like they're thinking of stopping. Not a minute later, he spots the cherry top of a Trooper car blazing in their direction. His first thought is the Trooper must have seen them and made a U-Turn.

His mind starts racing. He lowers his thumb out of the air. Shontay spots the car coming as well. She looks at Bugsy in suspense. He works his way over to the Lincoln, keeping his attention on the car which is approaching at a rapid speed. He positions himself behind the car as he draws both of his guns ready for war.

"Get behind me," he commands. "Get low!"

Shontay steps behind him in fear. "What you about to do?" she asks, knowing good and well what he has on his mind. "Bugsy, please think about this."

"Ain't nothing to think about," he said with a blank look on his face.

The Trooper's car approaches and to both of their surprise, passes them at about 90 miles an

n looking in their direction. They

gratitude.

iately tucks his guns into his

back to the shoulder. This time

ut his thumb, he flags traffic

ks back at Shontay who is just

ssly.

what the fuck? You just standing there looking pretty!" he shouts, taking his frustration out on her.

"What the fuck am I supposed to do?"

"Help me flag somebody the fuck down! That's what the fuck you can do!"

Shontay reluctantly walks over and put her thumb in the air. Together they stick out like two sore thumbs, but still no one attempts to stop.

Bugsy lowers his hand and looks over to Shontay with despair covering his face. "Ain't nobody in their right mind gonna stop with me out here. We got a better shot with just you," he figures. "I'm gon' sit in the car and maybe somebody will stop for you," he says as he steps toward the car. "At least you can use that pretty shit for something," he says with sarcasm.

He gets in the backseat of the Lincoln and lays low, hoping not to be seen.

Shontay stands on the curb flagging traffic down with a little more enthusiasm as Bugsy watches from the backseat. He holds his breath as an old white hillbilly in a pick-up truck bending his neck at Shontay as he passes her.

"Please, please," he mumbles to himself.

Shontay catches the man looking as well. She places her hands high in the air begging for him to stop. "Help me, please!"

The pick-up truck cuts a hard right onto the shoulder and slows down. The truck comes to a complete stop before it backs up at a moderate speed. The huge Confederate flag sticker that covers the back window captures Bugsy's attention. Bugsy, holds his breath until he sees the driver's door open and the old white man step out.

"Aye young lady, you okay?" the weird looking man asks. Perverted weirdo can be read on his face even in the darkness. "What's the problem?"

Shontay looks back at the car, waiting for Bugsy to step out and take the lead. The man looks into the car and spots Bugsy's head. He stops in his tracks. He fumbles for his waistband. In a second, he has a small pearl-handled handgun drawn and aimed. "I don't want no problems," he says, thinking it's all a set up.

"No," Shontay says, trying to reassure him.

Bugsy gets out of the car, hands in the air in submission. "It's not like that! Look my hands are in the air! We are really stuck! Can you please help us?" Bugsy holds his hands high. "Please?" he begs. "Our car just broke down on us."

The man backs away fearfully, gun still aimed at them. "I can't help you. I'll call the police for you."

"No! Please?" Shontay begs. "No police. Please help us?"

The old man trembles with fear. "Don't move or I will blow your nigger-ass brains out," he threatens. Prejudice bleeds from deep in his soul.

"Listen Sir, please just help us get our car started. I got money. How much you want?" If you let me go in my pockets, I will get my money. I'm reaching for my money," he says as he slowly puts his hand in his pocket. "I will pay anything if you can help me. I got a grand for you," he says as he holds a sloppy wad of money high in the air. "Here, you can have it all. I promise, this ain't no bullshit." The money attracts the old man. He stands there a little more at ease, but his gun is still aimed high. "What's the problem?" he asks.

"I don't know," Bugsy replies. "Please put the gun down?" Bugsy requests thinking of the attention they could be attracting to themselves.

The man's eyes are still glued to the money, he slowly lowers the gun. He takes a few steps toward them, watching them closely. "Here, I will put the money in your hand. Take it."

His greed overpowers the distrust. Hesitantly, he walks over, gun still aimed. He reaches for the money. "Come on, man, get that gun outta my face. Here go the money."

The man lowers the gun and snatches the money. He secures the money in his pocket before tucking his gun.

"Thanks," Bugsy says sarcastically.

"What's the problem?" the man asks while keeping his eyes on Bugsy's hands.

"I don't know. It just cut off on us. Luckily, we were in the slow lane and was able to cut over on to the shoulder."

"Cut off while riding? That has to be the alternator," the man claims. No disrespect, but can y'all both step to the back of the car while I take a look at it?"

"Psst," Bugsy says before stepping away. Shontay follows on his heels. As soon as both of them are at the trunk of the car, he looks under the hood and begins to bang away.

"Get in and try to start it up."

Bugsy hops in the driver's seat and twists the key in the ignition desperately. *Nothing...* He tries again and again with no success.

The man peers over the open hood. "That ain't your problem."

Bugsy gets out of the car. "Shit," he sighs. "What else can it be?"

"I don't have a clue."

"Here, take your money back. I can't help you. Call a tow truck," he says as he reaches into his pocket.

"Nah, we don't have time to wait for a tow truck." Thoughts of leaving the car enters his mind again. "Can you just get us off the highway? We will make it from there."

"I tell you what, maybe I can push you up a few miles. There's a rest stop with a mechanic on duty a few miles away up there in Baltimore."

Hope fills Bugsy and Shontay's heart. "Aye man, we would really appreciate that."

"Okay, come on," the man says as he steps toward his truck. Bugsy gets behind the wheel and Shontay dives in to the passenger's seat. The man backs his truck behind them and pulls close to their bumper.

"Drop it in neutral."

Seconds later, they're creeping along the shoulder at a turtle's pace. Their hearts are pounding faster than the car is moving.

TWENTY-THREE

The Maryland House / One Hour Later...

Bugsy and Shontay stand on the outside of the garage as the mechanic is under the hood of the Lincoln. They both stand there with the anxiety of a father in the delivery room. They pray that whatever the issue is, it can be resolved soon. They have no time to waste.

Twenty minutes later, the greasy mechanic walks out of the garage. They watch him with anticipation. "I got good news and bad news. Which one y'all want first?"

"Aye man, give me the bad news first," Bugsy replies.

The mechanic noticed the desperation in their eyes from the very start and he planned to capitalize off of it. "I'm a positive thinker so I like to deal with the positive first. The good news is I found your problem and the even better news is I just happen to have the part you need in stock." He hesitates before speaking. "The bad news is this isn't a cheap job. We have to take out the engine and that will take a couple of hours of labor. That will cost you a pretty penny."

"I got a pretty penny for the job so let's get it."

"Now, that's good news for me," the man smiles with a rotten toothed smile. "Now y'all go on inside and grab a bite to eat or something. I can't work with people watching down my back," he says without cracking a smirk.

Bugsy is hesitant to leave the car without supervision due to the contents of the trunk. "Now go on," the man commands.

Bugsy backpedals away with no rebuttal. He realizes the longer he procrastinates, the longer they will be stuck there. The State Trooper car that speeds past them motivates him to step away faster. They step toward the entrance of the building with no further hesitation.

Twenty Minutes Later...

Bugsy and Shontay occupy the window seats of Roy Rogers, eating and people-watching to blow the time away. A beautiful snow white S550, customized with shiny chrome rims pulls into a parking space right in front of them. Curiosity has them both watch as the driver of the Benz steps out of the vehicle. To both of their surprise, a casually dressed older gentleman gets out and makes his way toward the building. A brolic looking, clean cut man gets out of the passenger's seat.

They continue to watch the old man like a hawk as he steps in line and orders his food. He takes a seat across the aisle, without even taking notice of them. At nearly 60 years of age, he appears to have a swag that Bugsy can relate to. His designer driving loafers, gold Rolex and wood Cartier frames reek of money; old money.

The man picks up his phone and whispers into it with a suspicious demeanor as he discreetly observes his surroundings. He pays very little attention to them, although his partner watches them with a keen eye. Bugsy's gangster senses quickly identifies the brolic man as the old man's muscle; his bodyguard.

Not wanting to cause the men any concern Bugsy is mindful not to let them see him watching them. Through the corner of his eye he watches the man pick up his phone again while he peeks across the room out of the window. A triple black Ford pick-up truck cruises in to the parking lot. The truck parks right next to the old man's Mercedes.

The brolic man gets up from his seat and exits the building. Nosiness causes Bugsy and Shontay to shift their position in their seats and inconspicuously watch the brolic man. The older gentleman watches the outside activity closely as he nibbles on his food.

The brolic man gets in to the truck and in a matter of seconds, he gets out, holding a duffel bag. He peeks around cautiously as he steps to the Mercedes. Before he can get in, the truck peels off. The brolic man gets out of the Mercedes and comes back into the building. He takes his seat, and they both continue eating.

Bugsy stares at Shontay, with both of them well aware of what has just taken place. "Just as I figured. They just made a move right before our eyes."

Normally Bugsy would be thinking of a jack- move but today his mission is different. "I need to rap to them."

"For what?" she asks.

"We might just have what they need."

"We?" she asks sarcastically.

"Yeah, we," he replies. "Sha, you don't get it, huh? We both criminals," he says, further reminding her.

"You don't even know them. How you know what they just did?" she asks.

"I know they just made a move. What they moved, you're right, I don't know. But there's only one way to find out."

Bugsy's adrenaline races as the men get up from their seats, dumping the remains of their food into the bag. He can't let them get away from him. This feels like the chance of a lifetime that he can't let slip away. What he needs to say, he has not a clue, but he knows, he must say something. The men are now making their way out of the door. Bugsy gets up and starts walking, not knowing what he's about to say.

"Pardon me," he shouts, getting both of their attention. They stop at the door as he walks over to them. They both look at him with agitation on their faces. "I'm from outta state," he says as he fumbles for the right thing to say. "I got a question for y'all."

"Okay," the brolic man replies with tension building up on his face and in his voice.

"When the birds fly south for the winter where in Baltimore do they exactly land?" he asks with a spark in his eyes.

The spark in his eyes they both recognize. Neither of them say a word as they stare him up and down. They divert their attention to Shontay who sits idly, not even looking at them.

The old man finally speaks. "It all depends on how many birds are flying at a time, young fella. If they're flying in packs I just may know a few bird coops that they can rest in," he says cracking a grin.

Bugsy cracks a grin of satisfaction back at him. The tension between them dissolves. "I knew my senses weren't off. Is it possible that y'all could point me to the nearest pigeon coop then?"

The brolic man stares at Bugsy, trying to get a read on him. After his brief review, he looks over to the older gentleman with a sign. The older man nods his head.

"Absolutely."

TWENTY-FOUR

Hours Later...

Bugsy and Shontay have made the spacious and comfortable hotel room in downtown, Baltimore, their new temporary home. On the edge of the king size bed Bugsy sits as he breaks down and cleans not only his guns, but Shontay's gun as well. He has a practice of cleaning a gun after use. He has OCD when it comes to a weapon that he's fired, even if it' only been fired once. He doesn't trust a dirty gun and fears that in a crisis, the gun may misfire or jam up on him. Shontay leans propped, back against the headboard watching him.

"Babe, I think you should really think this out," she says. "You don't know these men from nothing and you're willing to risk everything by doing business with them."

"Sha, we saw them making a move with our own eyes. They're cokeboys," he says with attitude.

"They could be cops or even worse, feds. You don't what they're up to. You could be walking right into a set up. It's a huge chance that you're taking."

"All this shit has been a chance from the very beginning."

"Yeah, and look at where the chance has gotten us," she replies angrily.

"Yeah, well ain't no need to stopping now. We all the way in. Life is a chance! We take this chance and get rid of these last four birds and keep it pushing, loaded with money," he says as he looks into her eyes for the first time. "Or we sit back fiddling our thumbs and don't get rid of the work and we have to search throughout the city for buyers. Moving around in this city may just bring us more problems than we already have. This chance, I'm willing to take."

"From the beginning of this fiasco you have been dragging me along. I been at your mercy, just following your lead as you lead me to further destruction. Nobody can tell you nothing. You think you know everything and what I'm realizing is you don't know jack-shit!"

"I know more than you think I know. You textbook-school motherfuckers kill me, thinking you know every fucking thing! What, I don't know shit because I ain't college educated like you?"

"Where is that coming from?"

"It's coming from your smart-ass mouth! That's where! Always talking down to a mutha-fucka like you so smart. You a sheltered ass spoiled brat. That's what you are, always have been and always will be. You know what your school books taught you and the brainwashed shit the police academy taught you. You don't know shit about this life to tell me nothing about."

"Because this ain't my life. That's why!"

"Well, right now, this the fucking life we living! We are going to get with them dudes tomorrow morning and see what it's hitting for," he says as he loads the bullets into the magazine of her gun. He slams the cartridge into the gun in a rage. End of fucking discussion!"

TWENTY-FIVE

The Next Morning / 11:00 A.M.

Bugsy breaks a corner off the kilo and places it in a small baggie as Shontay watches him with fury. She doesn't have to say a word because her body language says it all. He wraps the Saran Wrap over the remainder of the kilo before dumping the baggie into his pocket.

"I'm not going," she utters as she walks across the room. He throws the kilo into the wall safe and slams the door. He storms behind her and snatches her by the collar. She snatches away from him. He grabs her by the back of her neck, pulling her closer and tighter. "Get your fucking hands off me," she says as she pulls away from him."

He's infuriated by her defiance. His anger gets the best of him and he can no longer control himself. He slaps her so hard she feels the impact of all of his frustration. The slap sends her sailing to the floor.

She sits there frozen and enraged for seconds as her face seems to distort like a character from an *Exorcist* movie. Bugsy has never seen anything like it. Her eyes become bloodshot red, and her lips snarl like she's possessed with a demon. She jumps up from the floor with no warning, gun already in hand.

Bugsy backs up in fear, stumbling against the wall. With her hand wrapped around his neck, she bangs her gun against his head. She's fed up with him. For the first time ever, she smells fear on him which gives her a feeling of domination that she's never felt. Thoughts of his abusiveness over the years fills her mind. Rage fills her heart as she thinks of how he's ruined her life.

"Put your hands on me again! she whispers demonically. Bugsy stands speechless. "Go ahead, and I will kill you in here. Go ahead, motherfucker," she dares as she nudges the gun against his head.

Bugsy stares into her eyes blankly. "You go ahead," he whispers. "Pull the trigger and end my life. Take me out of my misery."

She melts from the sound of his words. "I destroyed your life. I can't live with myself knowing that. You think this shit is easy for me knowing that?" he asks sadly. "Death would be easier," he says with sincerity. "Do me the favor and pull the trigger."

His words hit a soft spot in her heart, but seeing him in such a submissive state kind of turns her on. She feels a sense of control over him and she loves it. She squeezes his neck, slightly cutting off his circulation. As he tries to pull away from her grip, she taps his temple with the nose of her gun. He looks up at the gun before looking into her eyes.

"What?" she asks in mockery. "Say something."

He lowers his head in submission, not uttering a word. The sense of dominance she feels at this moment is orgasmic. She snatches him by his collar, pulling him off the wall. He allows his body to flop with each of her violent strokes with no fight at all. She slams him on the bed causing him to fall flat on his back. She walks over to him, slowly with her gun aimed at his head. She bites down onto her bottom lip sexily as fury bleeds from her eyes.

He stares up at her with confusion. She aims the gun at him with one hand as she unbuttons her dress with her free hand. She relaxes her gun hand just long enough to allow the dress to fall off her shoulders. As she aims the gun at his head once again, she places her thumbs along the waistband of her panties and wiggles out of them. As they hit the floor, she steps onto the mattress.

She stands over him. He stares upward at her nude body, totally ignoring the gun which is aimed at his face. She gently places the gun against his forehead. "Stop looking at me," she says before shoving his head back with force. "Close your fucking eyes."

Bugsy does as he's commanded to. He lays his head back onto the pillow. His manhood becomes as hard as the steel that rests against his forehead. Shontay notices his erection peeking up at her. She rubs her foot up and down the shaft over his jeans. "What the fuck is this? Did I tell you to get hard?" she asks as she taps the barrel of the gun against his face three times. With her toes, she traces little circles over the tip of his manhood, turning him on tremendously. His erection damn near busts through the denim. She stops the seduction and places the barrel of the gun onto his lips. "I didn't tell you that you can get hard."

Bugsy has always been superstitious-like. He hates for anyone to aim their fingers at him like a gun. He would never allow anyone to point a gun in his face whether playing or not. As uncomfortable as this may be for him, the sexiness of it all makes him forget all about his superstition.

With her two fingers, she closes both of his eyes. "Don't look at me." She steps closer to the bed, grabbing onto the headboard. Slowly, she squats down until her crotch is planted on his face. With the gun resting on his head, she grinds slowly, rubbing her lips over his lips. She grabs the back of his head and shoves herself onto him. She thrusts her hips with short pumps before gliding herself over his mouth.

She tightens her grip of his head and force-feeds the kitten to him. She holds his head tighter and tighter, almost suffocating him. He fights to pull away from her in order to get some air, but she applies all her weight on him, giving his face and nose no way to breathe. She smears her sex juice all over his face disrespectfully as he tries to pull away from her.

His fighting excites her to an all-time high. She places the gun on his forehead. "Make me cum," she whispers as she traces circles in the center of his forehead with the gun. She lifts up slightly, giving him some room to work. At the first touch of his tongue against her lips, she melts like putty as she always does.

As he French kisses her kitten, she leans her head back and enjoys the moment. He stops kissing it long enough to catch his breath. His tongue hangs from his mouth like a dog panting from thirst. The heat from his tongue attracts Shontay's kitten like a powerful magnet. She plants it on his tongue, not moving at all, just allowing the heat to melt through her walls.

She slides her twat over his whole tongue from the tip to the back, as close to his tonsils as she can get. She slides up and down on it like a sliding board. When she can no longer take the feeling, she uses his tongue as a trampoline, bouncing her clit up and down on it.

The intensity causes her to approach her climax in no time at all. In seconds, her entire body is ready to burst. She can no longer fight back the urge. She lets go and her insides explode before her walls cave in. Her juices erupt from within and seep into his mouth. He sucks the life out of her, making sure to get every drop that she has for him. Without realizing it, the gun has fallen out of her grip. She grabs his ears like handlebars as she rides his mouth, slowly, trying to calm her kitten.

Through his peripheral, he spots her gun lying next to him. His submissive demeanor is no longer. Like a madman, he lifts up from the bed, throwing her onto her back. She looks up at him with suspense in her eyes. He wraps his hand around her neck. With a gentle grip, he cuts of her air passageway.

Her claustrophobia kicks in causing her to freak out. She squirms and fidgets but can't get away from him. He tightens his grip as he unzips his jeans and pulls his manhood through the hole in his boxers. With his hand still gripped tightly around her neck, he allows himself to fall on top of her. He lifts her left leg high in the air before entering her. With great force, he drops himself into her balls deep, taking her breath away as he fills her up entirely. He pounds away, going deep with great force. She gasps for air as she tries to fight him off. He loosens his grip before changing up the tempo and slow stroking her in a teasing manner.

Shontay closes her eyes and drifts into euphoria. She's deep in La-La Land until all the pleasure is slapped out of her. Her eyes pop open and she stares at him in shock, not understanding what happened. He hauls off and slaps her once again before pounding away on her kitten abusively. Her gasping and moaning turns him into a sexual maniac.

Shontay is experiencing an out of body experience at this very moment. This whole ordeal has her somewhere far away on Fantasy Island. Bugsy draws his hand back and gives her the hardest slap of them all. She awakens from the fantasy with rage in her eyes until she spots her gun now in his hand. She can't help but notice his other hand on his rock hard manhood. He kneels before her with both guns aimed at her head. One gun fully loaded with deadly lead and the other fully loaded with hot passion.

He cracks a devious smirk at her. "It's all fun and games until the rabbit got the gun," he says as he taps her forehead with the gun. He erases the smirk quickly as he aims the gun at her head. "Now you make me cum."

One Hour Later...

They sit inside of the cozy little Seafood restaurant which is a few blocks away from the Harbor. Not until they got here, did they know that the restaurant belongs to the older gentleman, whom they now know as the General. In just a short time, they realize that the General is a major figure in this city.

The employees as well as the patrons treat him with the utmost respect. He reciprocates the respect, treating everyone as equals. He extends his hospitality to everyone. His etiquette is impeccable. A true gentleman he is. Judging by the way he maneuvers no one would suspect him to be a drug dealer. He carries himself like a successful legitimate businessman, a grandfather figure.

The General sits across the room from them eating from a hefty plate. The brolic man sits right next to him. Bugsy picks from his plate savagely, while Shontay sits staring at the wall with attitude blazing from her demeanor. The sexual escapade as pleasurable as it may have been, still didn't change her mind about this move. She wasn't with it before the sex, and she still wasn't with it afterwards. She opposes this ordeal with all of her heart.

"Hey young lady," the older gentleman says as he looks over his spectacles. "You're not hungry? You haven't touched your plate." Shontay ignores him rudely. "You know it's a disrespect to come here and not eat your food," he says with a smile. "You make me feel as if my food isn't good enough for you."

After realizing that he can't penetrate her anger, he looks over to Bugsy who shakes his head with a cheesy grin. "Women," he jokes. "Can't live with them, and can't live without them. Please don't mind her. It's not about you or your food. It's me that she's pissed with," he says as he nudges her with a stiff elbow, on the sneak tip.

"No offense taken. Well, without further ado, let's proceed with our business," he says as he looks over to Shontay. He gives Bugsy a head-nod, signaling him to excuse her.

"Oh naw, she good," Bugsy replies.

"I'm sure she is, but it's not my practice to discuss business in front of women. It's not gentlemen like, you know? The women's place is to look pretty and spend the money from the proceeds of the business," he says with a charmingsmile.

"It's okay though," Bugsy replies.

"No, I insist," he demands.

Bugsy turns to Shontay. "Sha..." Before he can finish his statement, she gets up from the table, knocking the chair on to the floor. The attention of the patrons is caught, and they all look over to their table. Bugsy wears an embarrassed look on his face. As he looks over, he notices the anger that's displayed on the brolic man's face. Bugsy flashes him a cold look back, engaging him in a staring battle.

Bugsy turns toward the General. "I apologize."

"No need to. I understand," he smiles. "Now, down to business."

Meanwhile...

The Peruvian housekeeper strolls the hall, pushing her cart full of cleaning supplies. She reads from her pad and stops at room 1012. The woman twists the knob and it opens. She knocks on the door.

"Housekeeping!" she shouts, knocking again. "Housekeeping!"

She steps into the room and peeks around, finding it empty. The sheets are ruffled at the bottom of the bed. The room reeks of the hot and steamy sex. She picks up the trail of dirty towels on her way to the bathroom. Once in the bathroom, she drops the dirty towels into her basket and begins tidying up.

Once the bathroom is done, she makes her way in to the bedroom. She snatches the television remote from the bed and aims at the television to shut it off. Her attention is then caught by the partly opened wall safe. Nosiness leads her over to it. She pulls it open and to her total surprise, she finds stacks of money as well as the drugs that she in no way is unfamiliar to.

Cocaine has been a part of her life for as long as she can remember. Her father was a kingpin and so were her uncles and her brothers. Kilos of cocaine were in the wide open in her house all her childhood, as if it was legal. She later fell in love with a drug dealer who she lost to the game by way of murder.

As common as drug dealing was in her family, she always hated it but accepted it as means of survival. It was a way of life for her family members, but not the way of life that she wanted for herself. After the death of her husband, she left Peru in search of a better life in America.

That better life that was promised to her has never come to fruition. Her role here in America has been cleaning dirty toilets from restaurants to bars. This job here is like a dream come true compared to the various other jobs that she's been forced to do just to make a living for herself and her six fatherless children.

Curiosity causes her to fumble through the stacks of money. As a child, her job was counting dirty money so she can do it in her sleep. She's been trained so well that she can listen to the sound of the bills flicking and decipher the ones from the fives, the fives from the tens and tens from the twenties. Through an expert eye, she approximates the money being well over two hundred grand.

Staring at the money and the four kilos, larceny creeps into her heart that she didn't know existed.

Larceny coupled with the pressure of the financial difficulty that she's under causes her for the one time in her life to think like a criminal. She quickly thinks of a cousin in New York that she can take the kilos to. Her mind takes her far away from Baltimore, Maryland. She envisions herself living lavishly in New York City, with a half a million in cash, living the American Dream as she pictured it to be. She stares in a daze just embracing the possibilities.

****

"So, you say you have only four left at the moment?" the General asks. "And then what? How fast can you have another supply? Or is this a one-time deal?"

"No, no, no," Bugsy replies, lying through his teeth. "I got the pipeline," he says bullshitting the General. He doesn't want the man to think he's a one hit wonder. "They come through ten, sometimes twenty at a time," he lies with a straight face. "The faster I move them, the faster they come back in."

The General is captivated. He can already see how much money he can make with the quality of work that Bugsy has shown him a sample of. "Make me one promise?"

"And what's that?" Bugsy questions.

"Make this your first and your last stop. I can't imagine my competition lucking up and coming across you. With me, you will have no need to look elsewhere. You've hit the jackpot. They don't call me the General for nothing," he says with a dazzling smile, exposing his pearly white dentures. "If you can guarantee me twenty a week, I can guarantee you that I will buy all twenty. Every week."

The big money talk that the General is doing triggers off dollar signs in Bugsy's head. For a second, he wonders what life would be like had he not murdered the Dominicans. They could supply him and he could supply the General. Scoring the five grand per kilo profit could land him a hundred grand a week profit, just dealing with the General. He's no scholar, but he can count and he estimates himself being a millionaire in just three months under different circumstances.

The fact that those circumstances don't exist, snaps him back into reality. If not for the murder of the Dominicans, he wouldn't be here in Baltimore, no way possible and he and the General would have never met. For a brief second, he regrets that it all played out the way it has. but it's way too late for regrets. He has to deal with what lies before him.

"So, you want all four?"

"Indubitably, I do," the General says with a smile.

"Tonight, I will put the paperwork together for you. I will call you bright and early in the am. We meet here. You bring the work, and I will have 160 grand for you. All large bills," he adds.

"One sixty?" Bugsy asks. "I told you forty-two a bird."

"What's a measly two thousand amongst businessmen? Young fella, don't look at it like you losing two grand. Look at it as a businessmen building a long lasting business relationship," he says with charm. "Look at it from a perspective of longevity. We will make millions together," he says before sitting in silence. "So, do we have a deal or do we have a deal?

Bugsy smirks before speaking. "Indubitably."

They shake hands over the deal. "I'm greatly pleasured to have you as my new business partner. Welcome to Baltimore."

TWENTY-SIX

Many Hours Later...

Bugsy stumbles in to the lobby of the hotel. He's been drinking like a fish since the end of his earlier meeting with the General. The mixture of drugs, alcohol and no sleep has him like a walking zombie. Shontay has to literally hold him up. She presses the elevator button as he leans against the wall for stability. A loud voice from behind him snaps him out of his high. "Freeze!"

He and Shontay turns around simultaneously. They both watch their freedom flash before their eyes as the lobby filled with a Swat team. There are more than twenty agents scattered around the room, all with their assault rifles aimed at them.

Pure reflex, intoxication and stupidity leads Bugsy to draw both of his guns with the quickness. Anyone who truly knows him, wouldn't expect anything less but his next move is the real shocker. He grabs Shontay by the neck and pulls her close to him. He places his gun against her temple. He scans

176

the room quickly and spots a sniper on the third floor with his gun resting on the railing. He thinks quickly. He plants his forehead against the back of Shontay's head.

"Back the fuck up!" he shouts as he hides behind her like she's a human shield. He flings her around aggressively. "Back the fuck up or I will spill her!" he threatens. "I already killed three of you pigs, so you know I don't have a problem killing another one."

Shontay is in total shock at him. "Baby, what are you doing?" she cries. "I'm with you. I'm on your side. Me and you against the world. It's over. The movie is over. The credits are rolling. Let's put our hands up and give up. Please baby," she cries in a low whisper. "I'm with you baby. How can you do this to me?"

"You're right baby. It's over, but I ain't going out like that. I ain't going to jail," he whispers in her ear.

"We will never make it out of here alive," she whispers.

"I ain't trying to make it out of here alive. My concern is you. This is your out."

"Please baby, don't kill me. Please," she begs.

"Sha, stop talking crazy. I would never kill you. I love you." He nudges her head with his gun, putting on a show for the agents. "You're innocent. It's me they want. Do what I tell you and you will be okay. Trust me on this," he says as he nudges her with the nose of the gun with force. "You have to give me up. Blame it all on me. Tell them I kidnapped you, forced you to come with me and I held you hostage all the way through. Tell them you feared for your life because I threatened you and your family."

More agents with guns pour into the lobby. They agents have them trapped. "This the end for me. Whatever you do, don't move. Keep your head right there," he says as he peeks up at the now three snipers whom are all aiming at him from different angles. "When this is over, you run to them Feds like you're happy to be finally free from me."

"Baby, what the fuck are you about to do? Please, just put your hands up and submit. We will fight our way out of this together."

"Shontay, it's over. I love you and I love my baby. Y'all go ahead and live happily ever after without me. I'm sorry about all of this," he says as a tear drops down his face. "Make all of it sound believable. Together we made a movie. Now go ahead and get our Oscar," he says as he sneakily lifts his gun and aims at the sniper. He fires with vengeance before a sniper on the left hits him with a fatal shot in the center of his forehead. The wind from the bullet blows past her ear, causing a whistling noise. In seconds, his body is riddled with over ten assault rifle bullets, killing him instantly.

"Get our Oscar," she hears clearly in her head. Without looking at his dead body, she takes off running with her hands still in the air. She doesn't stop running until she's in the arms of the first agent in the room. She hugs him tightly before falling onto the floor, sobbing away like a baby. Part of her is performing for the agents in order to retain her freedom. The other part of her is really happy that it's finally over.

Through her teary eyes, she watches as the agents' swarms Bugsy's lifeless body. Her fate she's still unsure of, until the agent lifts her on to her feet and walks her over to the couch. He sits her down comfortably.

"Officer Baker," he says.

Hearing the word officer gives her some hope. "Calm down, your nightmare is over."

TWENTY-SEVEN

Two Months Later...

The Peruvian woman pulls in to the parking space of the hotel. She gets out and walks into the building at the exact same time that she's been arriving for the past few years that she's been working there. To the naked eye, everything appears to be the same. No one would ever know that her life changed drastically two months ago. Thanks to Bugsy and Shontay, her financial situation has significantly improved.

For the first month, she lived with regret from her actions but her change of lifestyle erased her guilt. She did the right thing by notifying management, but what she didn't do was report all of her findings. She kept every dollar she found and the majority of the cocaine. She only gave them one kilo which she was sure was enough to get them arrested. The other three kilos, she took over to her cousin in New York who gave her seventy-five grand. A part of her felt horrible that Shontay and Bugsy's misfortune led to

180

her fortune, but thanks to them, she's finally living the American Dream that she originally came to the States in search of. Today she lives her life $400,000.00 richer.

****

Shontay walks out of the abortion clinic escorted by her sister. Guilt fills her heart as she thinks of the fact that she's just murdered her baby. That was one of the hardest decisions that she's ever had to make. It has taken her two months to finally go ahead and do it. All the way up until she laid on the table, she could hear Bugsy clearly begging her not to kill his baby. However, she knew that she had no choice.

The last thing she needs is for the authorities to get wind that she was pregnant. If she kept the baby, she feared that would blow her freedom. If they got wind that she was pregnant by the man who kidnapped her and she kept the baby, they may not believe the story that she fed them.

The past two months have been more hell for her than the few weeks of them being on the run. Seeing all that she's seen has altered her life dramatically. Her job forced her to seek psychiatric help to help her cope with the trauma. She only sought help to further make them believe her story, but once she got there, she realized that she really needed the help more than she knew.

After a few sessions, her psychiatrist would evaluate her and let the police force know if she's capable of performing her duty. With her job still on hold, she's really not sure if she wants to go back to it. She knows deep in her heart that she will never be the same person and may never be capable of performing her police duties. She also believes that even though they may have faked the world out, she will never be able to fool God. She believes her karma will be a wicked one. All she can envision is herself being killed in the line of duty and because of that, she no longer wants that duty. Shontay plops into the passenger's seat of her car while her sister starts the ignition. As soon as the car is on, the words of Jay-z and Beyoncé's *On the Run* blares through the speakers.

"Who wants that perfect love story anyway," Beyoncé's voice seeps through the speakers.

Bugsy quickly comes to mind. A series of their good times together pours into her mind and for a quick second, she actually smiles. That's something she hasn't done in months.

Over the months she's practiced forgetting about their bad times and only focusing on their good times. A few verses trigger her to start replaying the scenes of their crimes. *"I hear sirens as we make love,"* she whispers along with Beyoncé'. Scene by scene, of their adventure plays in her mind.

Her eyes water like a rainstorm as she sings along. *"I don't care if we on the run as long as I'm next to you,"* she whispers. *"They can take me... without you, I have nothing to lose,"* she shouts aloud, causing her sister to look at her.

Shontay quickly snaps herself out of the zone. She quickly switches the station to remove those scenes from her head. All of this is one big disastrous memory that she wishes to no longer remember.

THE END

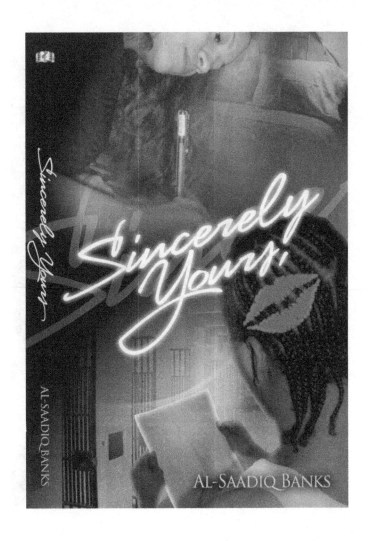

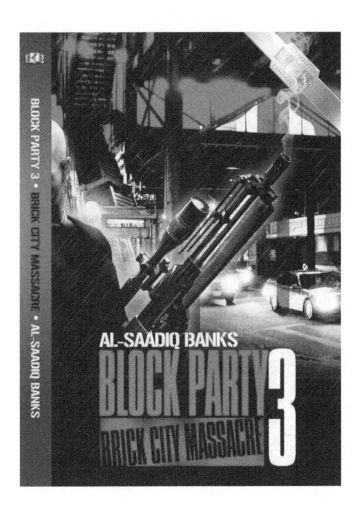

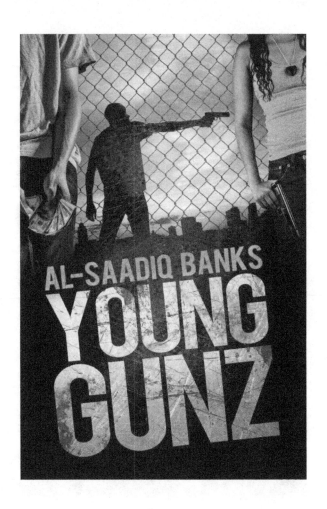

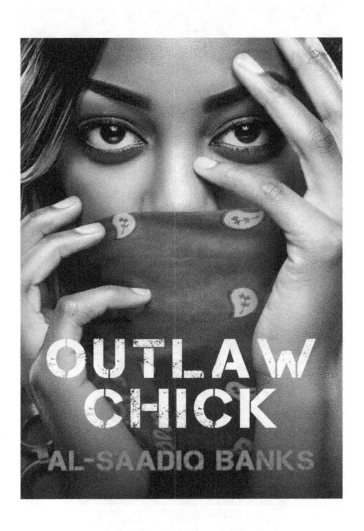

BOOK ORDER FORM

Purchaser Information

Name: _____

Address: _____

City:_____ State: _____ Zip Code: _____

$14.95 - No Exit ___

$14.95 - Block Party ____

$14.95 - Sincerely Yours _____

$14.95 - Caught 'Em Slippin' _____

$14.95 - Block Party 2 ____

$14.95 - Block Party 3 ____

$14.95 - Strapped ____

$14.95 - Back 2 Bizness (Block Party 4) ____

$14.95 – Young Gunz _____

$14.95 - Block Party (Comic)____

*$14.95 – Block Party 5 - 5k1.1 - Diplomatic Immunity
*Coming fall of 2015

14.95 + 1.04 = 15.99 per book. Shipping is 5.75 for up to 3 books. Each additional book is 1.00 extra for shipping. Orders of six or more books shipping is free.

Make Checks/Money Orders payable to:

True 2 Life Publications *- PO Box 8722 – Newark, NJ 07108*